Bossed Up with a
REAL ONE
A Thug's PASSION

A NOVEL BY
SADE IONA

Royalty Publishing House is now accepting manuscripts from aspiring or experienced urban romance authors!

WHAT MAY PLACE YOU ABOVE THE REST:

Heroes who are the ultimate book bae: strong-willed, maybe a little rough around the edges but willing to risk it all for the woman he loves.

Heroines who are the ultimate match: the girl next door type, not perfect - has her faults but is still a decent person. One who is willing to risk it all for the man she loves.

The rest is up to you! Just be creative, think out of the box, keep it sexy and intriguing!

If you'd like to join the Royal family, send us the first 15K words (60 pages) of your completed manuscript to submissions@royaltypublishinghouse.com

SYNOPSIS

Can you be a successful businesswoman, a sister, and have a relationship?

For Ever, Raye, and Taylor, that is the question these three sisters ask themselves daily while harboring a deadly secret. Ever is the oldest and has made it her mission to always protect her sister. But with the pain she's endured in the past, will she able to open herself up to love again? Raye is used to turning up. She never requires much from a man, taking the bare minimum of whatever it is they give her. Will she be able to notice a real man when he presents himself to her, or will she be so used to untrustworthy guys that she'll miss out on real love? Taylor loves to burn sage and work on her inner peace. But with the pain she encounters in her childhood, she has shunned relationships altogether until she meets someone worth loving.

Being on top has its highs and lows. And Benny, Lake, and Tru know that all too well. With very little family, they are bonded by their loyalty and love for each other. Benny has lost more than most, but still, he finds a way to reign on top with his brothers. But will a chance encounter with a girl in the club leave him getting more than he thought?

Lake has always been the chill one out of the group, focusing on raising his daughter and keeping his baby's mother in check. Can someone help bring some peace to his already dysfunctional life? Tru always speaks his mind. Running a successful drug business with his brothers, he has to keep a flock of bitches on deck, but when he sees a familiar face in the crowd, he knows that there's more to her.

Take a ride with these characters and their journey through life and see who really is riding with their shooter.

DEDICATION

This book is dedicated to all the girls out there who grew up reading the classics. I'm talking The Coldest Winter Ever and Flyy Girl type shit. I hope to be there one day and leave an impact on people's lives as those stories did to mine.

ACKNOWLEDGMENTS

Special shoutout to Darryl & Legend Brooks. Thanks for helping me find myself!

Enjoy!

CHAPTER 1

Ever

"Will y'all stop fussing, and let me be?" Grandma Tottie swatted us away with her cane. We watched our grandmother as she struggled in pain to make it across her bedroom. Even with just having surgery a few days ago, she refused to be treated as someone incapable of doing for themselves.

It had been her fourth stroke in six months. My sisters and I had moved up from Atlanta to New York to look after our grandmother. Of course, she put up a fight the whole way, but there was no way that we would leave Grandma Tottie up her by herself.

Before I continue, let me introduce myself. My sisters will do the same as well. I'm Ever Jones, twenty-three, and the oldest of my sisters, Raye and Taylor, by a year. We were originally from Brooklyn, New York, but our parents moved us down south some years back. It'd been three months since we moved back to take care of Grandma Tottie, and she'd been fighting us every step of the way.

"Wait, Grandma. Let me help you." Taylor tried to reach for my grandmother's arms because she was struggling to get up, but Taylor was met with the handle of her cane to her head.

"What I done told y'all girls already? I'm old, not helpless. By God, I love ya, but y'all is driving me crazy. Dick blocking me and stuff," her little cute, fresh self said.

Grandma Tottie was eighty-one years young and had aged so gracefully. Her thick, gray, shoulder-length hair swung loose. Her smooth, mocha skin always smelled like coconuts, and her hazel eyes that I inherited told her story.

"Ouch! You lucky I love you, lady, 'cause there's some things I would do to someone who hit me with a cane that wasn't my favorite grandma," Taylor joked as she rubbed the spot where Granny's cane had hit her.

"Come on, y'all. Let her get some rest." I came up on the side of her king-size bed and laid a bunch of kisses on her face. My sisters followed suit before closing the door to her bedroom.

We had purchased Granny a five-bedroom, three-story brownstone located in the heart of Brooklyn. She loved to look out her window. Grandma always had the latest neighborhood gossip.

"Raye, has Carlos made any more calls?" I asked as she took a seat on the couch right next to me in the living room while Taylor's weird ass lay on the carpet floor.

"No, but I put trackers on it to alert me when he does. I also put alerts on all his bank accounts and his offshore accounts with that little ass mill in there he thinks no one knows about. I know his dumb ass is gonna slip up soon. This is too easy." Typing away in her MacBook, she went to work.

One of the things that I loved about my sisters was that we were all fucking great at something. Raye was a beast with her hacking shit. Taylor was obsessed with cars; that came in handy. And me—well, let's just say guns were my specialty.

"Good. Keep me up to date if there's any movement on his shit." Standing up, I stretched and yawned. I was beat and ready for bed. We had just gotten back in the country from a business trip, and I wanted nothing more than to lay up in my bed with a bag of popcorn. "See y'all tomorrow," I started to tell them while turning to walk away toward my bedroom.

"Oh, hell no, bitch. You can't be deadass. Ever, it's Saturday! We are about to get lit. Grandma Tottie is good, so we are going out," Raye said while grabbing my arm to prevent me from leaving.

CHAPTER 2

Raye

OK, let me get this shit out the way. I'm Raye. Let's just say I was the fun one; I liked to have a good time, and I loved hanging out with my sisters... Well, it wasn't like I had friends anyway. I had to look away so I wouldn't laugh at Ever's old lady ass, who looked uncomfortable being in the club.

I had to literally drag my sister out of the house tonight, and I was so glad I did. She looked so beautiful, and she didn't even know it. Nah, she did. Ever had on a sparkly see-through top that glistened on her mocha skin and paired ut with some distressed jeans with her thick thighs peeking through, and her big, curly afro that she dyed honey-blonde made her hazel eyes pop more.

Sipping on Moët, I bopped to the music as I watched Taylor come back with her third shot. Just like Ever, Taylor and I were both in sparkly pieces. She had on a sparkly bralette with loose, black, leather jeans, looking every bit like Aaliyah. Her caramel skin and her bone-straight, jet-black hair just put her fit together.

"Raye, you gotta let me borrow that dress," Taylor said as she took a seat next to Ever in our VIP section in 40/40. I wasn't one to brag, but I was looking like the shit. I had on a halter-top sparkly dress that stopped right above the knee. My blonde pixie cut was in some cute finger waves that made my freckles that graced my face stand out even more.

"Yeah right. I'm still waiting for your ass to give me back my Givenchy dress," I said, giving her the side-eye. Taylor blew me a kiss.

"Oh shit, the Vale Boys are in the building! Move the fuck out the way!" the DJ yelled through the club. As if on cue, the crowd started to part as a group of niggas made their way to the VIP next to us.

"Who the fuck are these niggas? I been hearing their name since we got up here." I looked their way, and Ever and Taylor both shrugged their shoulders, just as clueless as me.

"Said little bitch, you can't fuck with me if you wanted to. These expensive. These is red bottoms. These is bloody shoes. Hit the store, I can get 'em both. I don't wanna choose, and I'm quick to cut a nigga off, so don't get comfortable. Look, I don't dance now; I make money moves," my sister and I sang along as we got up from our section and onto the dance floor.

Even Ever's old lady ass started winding and bobbing to the music. These were the moments I lived for—just having fun and enjoying life with my sisters. While still on the dance floor, I couldn't help having the feeling that I was being watched. Granted, we were turning up, and people were looking, but this felt like someone was looking through my soul.

Scanning the VIP section, I looked to the area where the Vale Boys' crew was posted up. That's when I saw three niggas posted up in VIP, and I kid you not, none of them were ugly. They each had thirsty ass bitches in their faces, but then I saw him. He had his hair in a bun, a freshly cut goatee paired with a low beard, and his neck covered in tats, and he almost looked as if he were Indian or something.

"Raye, come on. We going to the bathroom." Ever grabbed my hand, making me break my stare down with the mystery guy.

CHAPTER 3

Benny

From the moment I saw her enter the club, I knew I wanted her. She looked annoyed as hell, being in this packed-ass club with thirsty niggas in every corner. I wasn't gonna lie; ma was looking real right with thick thighs and a curly fro. She seemed so alert as she scanned the club as if she were looking for anything out of the ordinary.

"Benny, why the fuck you are staring at that bitch!" Tracey yelled at me over the loud music. Let a bitch hang with you in VIP, and she thought she was your girl or some shit.

"Yo, Tray, on some G shit, don't get fucked up, questioning me about who the fuck I'm staring at with my own two fucking eyes!" Frustrated, I reached for the whole bottle of Rosé and guzzled it down.

We were out getting lit, per usual, and Lake's dumbass thought it would be a good idea to bring some thots with us. Looking over at Tru's ass, who was having a stare down with shawty that came with lil' momma that I was plotting on, I could do nothing but chuckle at how hard he was staring at shawty.

"Nigga, you might as well call lil' momma and her girls over. The way y'all staring at each other and shit," I said.

"Man, shut up. She looked familiar. I just don't know from where... Shit, she bad too though." Rubbing his beard, he once again turned his head in their direction.

"We can head back to your place after. I don't mind spending the night," Tracey said, caressing my back as I watched lil' momma and her girls head toward the restroom while dodging niggas in the process.

"Man, listen. If we go back to my place, the only thing we are doing is fucking." Guzzling the last of my drink, I tuned her ass out and bobbed my head to the music.

CHAPTER 4

Taylor

Guess it's my turn now. Hey, I'm Taylor. I was the laid-back one. Ever was the old lady, Raye was the turn-up queen, and I was just like chill. That's probably why when Raye told us about some dude that was staring at her, all I could think about was wishing I brought some more weed with me.

"Taylor, your high ass probably ain't even hear a word I said," Raye fussed as she washed her hands and checked herself out in the mirror. Ever had wanted to make sure Grandma Tottie was OK, which she found out she was once she cursed Ever's ass out on the phone.

"Yeah, I did. Some guy was staring at your beautiful ass, and you acting all scared." Playfully shoving her, I reached for my phone to take a selfie before giving my attention back to Raye.

"It's not that. I don't know. I can't explain it. Just forget about it. But damn, he looked good... Shit, they all did," she said as we exited the bathroom and made our way back to our section. Looking in the direction of the guys that Raye had pointed out earlier, I couldn't lie; they all did look fine. I didn't know what came over me, but I was feeling myself and wanted to go and approach one of them.

"Bet you I can get them to come over here." Grinning at my sisters, I adjusted my breasts before walking over to their section.

"Umm… can we help you? Is your ass lost?" a pretty, dark-skinned girl with a gap in the middle of her front teeth asked nastily. See, I said I was the chill one but not to bitches who got out of pocket.

"Actually, no you can't, space gap, but he can," I said, pointing to the one whose lap she sat on. His green eyes were low, so I was sure he had just smoked some good shit. Brushing his golden dreads from out of his face, he smiled at me. I even had his boys' attention. I wasn't feeling too bold as he stared at me with those green, cat-like eyes.

"How so, ma?" his cute, light-skinned ass asked me while licking his plump pink lips. Shit, I was so high I couldn't even think of an excuse.

"Umm… my sisters. Yeah… can you take a picture of me and my sisters for me?" I asked while pointing to the section that my sisters were staring back at us from.

"Y'all sisters?" cutie with the man bun asked while looking behind me to look my sisters' way again. Nodding my head, I looked back at the dread head and waited for him to reply.

"No, he can't. You better ask someone else, hoe. Fuck you think this is, bitch?" gap tooth asked, rolling her eyes.

"You're such a pretty girl. I would hate to see your skull smashed in because of your mouth," I said, moving closer to her. Standing up, dread head got in between us.

"Damn, shawty, that turned dark." He laughed while grabbing my hand. Gap tooth looked tight, but for some reason, I knew she wasn't gonna get crazy about it.

"Yo, Lake, hurry up, man. We 'bout to dip soon," the quiet one of the group said while turning his attention back to the light-skinned chick in his lap. I took in his clear, brown skin, low-cut waves, and the most defined jawline ever. He just had to be a model; that nigga was beautiful.

"Hey, y'all, this is, um… Lake. He gonna take that picture for us." I nervously smiled at my sisters, who looked lost for a second before catching on and nodding their heads in agreement. Handing him my phone, we all stood close together and posed for the picture.

"OK, Lake, I have to get one with you for being so nice." Handing my phone to Ever, I stood by Lake.

Taking me by surprise, he pulled me from behind, and I felt his dick press against my butt. Grinning, we posed for the picture.

"I got to get going, but I put my number in your phone. Hit me up," he said while waving to my sisters. Stopping midway, he circled back. Thinking he dropped something, I didn't think much of it 'til he stopped in front of me.

"I forgot to ask your name." He smiled, showing all thirty-two of his straight pearly whites.

"Taylor. This is Ever and Raye," I said, pointing at my sisters who sat nearby.

"Alright, Ms. Taylor, see you around." He looked me up and down once more before joining his friends and leaving.

CHAPTER 5

Benny

"Jose, this is the last dropoff I'm doing with your fat ass," I said, taking the last bit of shipment from the van. Walking into our warehouse with Jose's fat ass right behind me, I got tight all over again. I had been in this drug game long enough to know that beyond being feared in the streets, niggas had to also respect you. And looking at this fat, sloppy motherfucker standing in my face instead of my usual connect Carlos had me on ten.

"And where the fuck is Carlos at anyway? Why the fuck he ain't here? Tell Carlos that if his ass ain't at the next drop off, we gonna have a problem."

Jose's fat ass wiped the sweat dripping from his forehead while looking back at me nervously. "Benny, you know Carlos loves doing business with you, man. And he told me to let you know that he will definitely be at y'all next meeting," he said.

I had been doing business with Carlos for a few years now, and for some reason, he just stopped coming to any of our meetings. I was a fucking boss, and I'd be damned if I continued to do business with his fat ass flunky Jose.

"Man, if that nigga Carlos wasn't supplying us with the best coke right now, I would have said we should off that nigga," my bro Tru said as he sat on one of the random couches we had in the warehouse. See, Carlos had been hooking us up with the best coke from Columbia, which was hard as fuck to get.

"Yeah, I know, bro, but you already know we ain't gonna have to be dealing with that shit much longer," I said.

"Yo, we gotta get out of here now if we gonna catch this game," Lake came up and said. For the past three years, we had been sponsoring basketball tournaments in Brooklyn. We gave prizes, paid for kids' jersey, and shit, if any of the little niggas needed money for food, they knew we had them.

"Ayo, Tone, make sure dem niggas get their shit by the end of the day," I ordered one of my hitters before leaving out.

～

SUNSET PARK...

"Yeahhh, Kev, that's how you do that shit!" I yelled as one of my little niggas on my team scored a three-pointer. Taking in my surroundings, I peeped Lake's ass cheesing on his phone.

"Fuck you over there cheesing about? Over there like a female."

"Shit, B, you know that's probably Kim's crazy ass asking for another chance and telling him how good she'll fuck him," Tru's dumbass said before Lake came up behind him and put him in a headlock.

"Man, fuck y'all. I ain't even fucking with Kim like that if it ain't 'bout my daughter. Nah, that was shawty from the club a few weeks back," he said as Tru got out of the headlock, and they started play fighting. "Man, remember the chick that asked me to take a picture for her? Had me being a photographer? And my dumbass did it."

Little did he know, I was already plotting on how to get lil' momma's info. Ever since I saw her in the club, she'd been on my

12

mind heavy. I didn't know what the fuck was going on with me, because a bitch could barely hold my attention for a minute.

"I'm surprised your rude ass ain't tell her to suck your dick when she asked you that shit." Tru chuckled a bit, and I drew my attention back to the game. My little niggas were up by twenty.

"That's the thing, bro. I do want her to suck my dick and then have my babies," his dumbass said.

*

CHAPTER 6

Tru

"This nigga stupid," Benny said as we all broke out in laughter. Ever since I could remember, Lake's ass had always said some dumb shit. Benny, Lake, and I had been tight since we were little niggas. We are the closest thing to family we had, and I would never turn my back on them for anything.

"Heyyy... Tru, when you gonna come over again?" Asia's thick ass asked me as she walked up with her chickenhead friends. See, I had a team of bitches I kept on call. But when bitches forgot their place or thought more of something than what it was, I had to cut them off.

"When your ass learns your place. Asia, you ain't my girl, so you thinking it's OK for you to fight and question any bitch I'm with is a problem to me. You lucky I'm trying out this nice shit, or else I would have just killed your ass." I looked her in her eyes so she wouldn't doubt for one second that I was serious.

"Tru, please. I'm so sorry..."

Fuck anything Asia was talking about. My attention, along with every other nigga on the courts, was on the three beautiful women that just walked into the basketball tournament.

The one that looked like Aaliyah had on a Calvin Klein bra with some loose-fitting jeans. Little momma was small but most definitely curvy. Shit, all three of them looked no taller than five feet, if that. The other pretty one with the big fro had a denim dress with no bra on that showed off her perky breast and nice, thick, brown thighs, and she paired it with those Rihanna sneakers that Asia's ass begged me to get her.

Then my eyes landed on the one with the short, blonde hair and those pretty ass feckless. She looked so familiar; I just couldn't figure out from where. She had on an off-the-shoulder crop top with some short ass jean shorts and a pair of 11s on her small ass feet.

"Damn, Tay, you gonna make me shoot a nigga for looking at you too hard," Lake said as he pulled his girl in for a hug. Benny and I got up from our seats on the bench so that her sisters could sit down.

"These my bros, Benny and Tru," Lake introduced us.

"Hey, these are my sisters, Ever and Raye," she said as our team scored the final point and won the game.

"You got some nice ass hair," Raye said as she ran her long red fingernails through my hair.

Depending on how I felt, my hair would be braided straight back one day, in a bun the next, or like today, I just let that shit hang loose. But what I didn't fucking tolerate was bitches touching me without my permission. That's probably why Benny and Lake were looking at me worriedly. I usually would have smacked the shit out of a bitch for touching me without my permission, but like I said, I was trying out this being nice shit.

"Thanks, ma. I need to get this shit braided up though," I said, looking into her soft brown eyes.

Licking her clear glossy lips, she said, "Well, I know how to braid, so whenever you ready, I can do it for you."

I nodded my head because the furthest thing from my mind was her braiding my hair, but if that's what it was gonna take for me to get in between her legs, then so be it.

"I guess I'mma have to take you up on that offer, Raye." Tucking in my bottom lip, I watched her turn a little red and giggle.

CHAPTER 7

Lake

"Yo, I'mma be right back. I'mma get some more Kush from my car." Pulling up my Nike Techs, I grabbed Taylor by the hand, taking her with me.

"You betta not try nothing with my sister, Lake," her pretty but mean ass sister with the fro said. Taylor and I just laughed at her mean ass as we walked out the courts.

"Oh shit, you got a Koenigsegg One!" Taylor yelled. Shit, she had me surprised that she even knew what type of car this was. Most females wouldn't. I lifted up the passage side door for her before sliding into the driver side.

"Let me find out you know some shit about cars. This shit cost me a million dollars, but it goes fast as fuck, though." Taking out the weed from my glove box, I started breaking it up.

"Trust me, I know. Shit, I was about to get me another one... I mean, I always wanted one." She nervously laughed. I didn't know what came over me, but I just wanted to see her smile all the time.

Taylor was a good girl in school for engineering and taking care of her grandmother and shit. I was so used to bird bitches that didn't have shit going for themselves but were just good for sucking dick.

Lighting up the blunt, I took a couple of pulls before passing it over to Tay.

"You like that shit. That's blue dream," I said, watching Taylor cough a little. Before she could reply, my phone began ringing and displaying my baby mama's name.

"What bitch is you with at the courts, Lake!" Kim's crazy ass yelled as soon as I answered the phone.

Wiping my hand down my face, I was already about ten seconds away from going off on her simple ass.

"Is Ava OK?" I asked her about our daughter as I glanced toward Taylor who smiled lightly at me. Damn, I hoped I didn't scare her ass off with my baby mama bullshit.

"Nigga, you got me fucked up out here." See, Kim had me all the way fucked up.

See, there were a few things I regretted in my life, and Kim was one of them. Don't get me wrong; I loved the fuck out of my daughter, Ava, but her mama was foul. About a year ago, we threw Benny a loft party for his birthday. Kim was one of the strippers we had hired. My ass got so fucked up that I fucked up, and I got her ass pregnant. After DNA proved Ava was mine, Kim's life was spared, but she was making that shit hard as fuck.

"Kim, I'm only gonna ask one more time before we have a problem. Is Ava OK?" The seriousness in my voice had her ass on mute for a minute.

"Yeah, she is, but—"

Before she could say anything else, I hung up on her simple ass. Breathing out, I put my hand on Taylor's thigh. "Sorry about that. I had to make sure my daughter was OK," I said to her, hoping she'd still fuck with a nigga.

"Lake, you don't have to explain shit to me when it comes to your daughter. As long as your baby mother knows her place, then we cool." Showing off her deep ass dimples, she smiled. I just knew she was gonna be my weakness.

"Good. I ain't want you to run without at least sampling this dick," I said, grabbing my semi-hard dick while grinning at Taylor.

"Trust, I will sample the D once we go on a date first," she said as I started my car up. I was about to pull off.

"Lake, no, silly. I can't leave my sisters. Plus, I gotta get cute first." Taylor laughed as we got out of the car and went back to the courts.

CHAPTER 8

Ever

*I*t was nice seeing young black boys out there doing something positive. Most young men in this area usually joined gangs, ended up in jail, or died. It was becoming hard to focus on the game with Benny staring right in my face. Raye's ass was all up in Tru's face, so I didn't have anyone to talk to.

"You look all stiff and shit over there, ma. Relax. Ain't nobody gonna hurt you." Benny chuckled while he stood next to me, watching the next game began. He had been staring at me with those light-brown eyes since the moment we came. I usually didn't get shy, but with him, I could barely focus on the game.

"Trust me, I know ain't no one gonna hurt me. I just don't wanna be here." I was trying my hardest not to look at his handsome face or those deep, light-brown eyes of his. From the moment we walked up, all I saw was him. His presence alone did something to me. I hadn't really given guys any thought for a while… until now.

"Well, shit, leave then 'cause you fucking up my high," he said with his handsome face all twisted up. Annoyed, he walked away from me.

One thing I hated the most was when someone walked away from me, especially when I wasn't done talking.

"Ever, let it go, sis," Raye tried to reason with me, but it was too late; my feet were already hitting the pavement.

I walked up to where Benny had some basic ass hood bitch with a blonde wig on in between his legs, and he was sitting on the hood of an all-white Bentley Bentayga like it was a fucking regular car.

Who the fuck were these niggas? I had to get Raye to do a background check on them.

"I wasn't done talking to your ass, Benny," I said, walking up to them with an attitude. I didn't even know why I was so pissed off. Shit, maybe I just wanted to find any excuse to keep talking to him.

Pushing the blonde-haired bitch off of him, he was in my face with the quickness. I didn't realize how tall he was until he was towering over me. He had to at least be six feet three easy. Damn, he smelled good.

"You don't know me, and that's the only reason your ass is getting a pass for the disrespect. But you won't be so lucky again," he threatened me, taking me out of my thirsty thoughts.

I pushed him back a little. "No, nigga, you don't know me. Don't let this cute face fool you, Benny. I can be just as dangerous."

This nigga had the nerve to smirk and lick his lips. "Yeah, you definitely gonna be mine," he said.

I just walked away, leaving him standing there and me with soaked panties.

CHAPTER 9

Taylor

"Alright, y'all, how I look?" I walked into the kitchen, and my sisters were sitting at the table while Grandma Tootie finished making her some tea. I did a little spin, showing off my curves in my fitted Balenciaga floral jumpsuit while my hair hung straight with a middle part.

"What y'all be saying? You are looking like a snack, sis," Grandma Tootie said, giving her best impersonation of Raye. You couldn't tell her that she wasn't hip. My sisters and I had tears in our eyes because she was serious.

"Well, thanks, girl. I get it from you." Hugging her from behind, I took in her coconut scent and thought about how close we came to her not being around.

"Yeah, Taylor, you look pretty. You have your thing on you?" Ever's overprotective ass asked, referring to my Glock 17 she had given to me on my birthday last year.

"Oh my God, Ever, yessss! Stop worrying so much. Lake isn't gonna hurt me. Plus, if he does, I know y'all will kill that nigga for me," I said to her.

"Taylor, you know I'll do more than just kill him. I just want to make sure that you are on your guard. We don't know these niggas. That's all I'm saying," she said, coming up and kissing me on the cheek.

"I'll get the wine. Raye, get the popcorn. Taylor leaving us to go get some dick." My sisters laughed, leaving out of the kitchen to Ever's room.

Before I could respond, my phone buzzed with a text from Lake.

Lake Baby: *I'm outside. Wnt me to come and get u?*

Me: *Nah heading out now.*

"OK, y'all, I'm leaving. Don't wait up." After kissing everyone one last time, I was on my way out the door.

"Aww, Lake, I'm so full." I kicked off my heels as soon as we entered into Lake's condo in New Jersey. He had taken me to a place called Soco, and let me tell you, they had the best red velvet chicken waffles hands-down.

Over dinner, I found out a lot about Lake, especially how his baby mama basically trapped his ass, but there was no denying his love for his daughter.

Even though Ever always warned us about keeping our guard up with new people, I could feel them falling for him.

"Shit, you better be. You ate most of my food too." Picking up my feet, he slowly massaged them.

My feet looked so tiny in his massive hands. My foot massage was feeling so good, and Lake looked even better. His dreads were neatly retwisted and put into one big braid. He had on a red graphic Gucci hoodie with some black sweats and some wheat Timbs. Everything about him was so damn sexy to me.

"Fuck you over there drooling about, Tay Baby? I ain't even put it on ya yet." Placing my feet on the floor, he grabbed my hand and headed toward his bedroom. His bedroom was simple with a big ass California king bed, and a few candles added a sweet scent to it. "I been wanted to taste you since your goofy ass asked me to take a picture for you," he said.

"Well, shit, go ahead. I ain't gonna stop you." I helped him help me out of my jumpsuit.

As he kissed me lightly on my lips, I sucked on his bottom lip before licking it and letting go. He started making a trail of kisses from my head all the down to my kitty.

"Damn, Tay Baby, your shit looks so pretty. I don't know what the fuck is up with me. I ain't never wanted the pussy so bad," he said to himself before feasting on me. The way his long, thick tongue glided up and down my pussy lips had me ready to explode.

"Mmmh... Lake, shit." He had two fingers in me while he nibbled on my clit. "Lake, I'm about to..." I came harder than I ever had in my life.

Giving my kitty one last kiss, he came up for air with my sweet pussy juices all over his plump pink lips.

Stroking his dick had me literally drooling at the size and thickness of his ten-inch dick. His shit had a slight curve that I knew was about to fuck my whole life up.

"You OK, Taylor?"

I nodded my head quickly because I just needed the dick now.

"Shit, ma, your shit soaking wet." As he dove in and out of me, the only sounds were my wetness and moans.

I COULDN'T DO anything but smile when I rolled over in bed with Lake lying beside me. If you had told me that I would be willing to give my all and commit to a nigga, I would have probably run your ass over.

Out of my sisters, I was the one that feared relationships and never really had a boyfriend. I guess I was always afraid that I would give my love to someone that would just leave like my... Nope, I didn't even want to think about it.

"Why your creepy ass smiling at me while I'm sleeping?" Lake asked with his eyes still closed.

"Boy, bye. I was just making sure none of that stink slob got on my hair," I said.

"Yeah right. I know I got your ass feeling butterflies right now."

Punching his arm, I got up and went to brush my teeth.

About two hours and three sex sessions later, Lake and I had finally managed to get dressed and eat.

"So, tell me something about you that no one knows," he said while we sat down at his table, eating our cold breakfast.

"Umm, there isn't really much to tell. Go to work, school, and take care of my grandmother," I answered quickly.

"Bullshit, Tay Baby. I'm good at reading people, and your eyes is telling on you."

I looked at his face, seeing that he really was not about to drop the subject. "OK, fine. I'll tell you something only my sisters and parents know about me," I finally said.

Bronx, NY 2001...

"I'm tired of this, Travis! If you ain't at work, you just giving all your attention to her," my mom said, pointing her finger toward my tiny face.

This wasn't something new. My momma was always arguing with my daddy, mostly about me. My daddy, Travis Brown, was my hero and best friend. I was a daddy's girls in every sense. Where he went, I went.

He would even take me to work with him at the auto repair shop. I guess that's where my love for cars came from. But for as long as I could remember, my mom didn't really care much for me. She didn't beat me or anything, but she acted jealous as if I were taking her man from her or something.

"What the fuck you mean, Roxy? That's our daughter!" my father yelled back at her. My dad's handsome face was balled up into a look of disgust. He picked me up from the corner where I had been crying and kissed my cheeks.

"No, Travis, she's your daughter. And you just gonna have to choose—me or her," she said, looking at me with hate in her eyes as she waited for him to respond.

"Then I choose my daughter every time." He turned with me still in his arm, about to reach for the door handle.

"If you leave out of here with her, I'll call your P.O., Travis!" my mom yelled out. Gently placing me down, he hemmed up my mother in a second.

"Roxy, you must have forgot who the fuck I really am! Bitch, don't let the new me fool you; I'm still that savage ass nigga." Grabbing her tightly by the face, he stared into her eyes before letting go. Kneeling down in front of me with those soft eyes, he kissed my cheek.

"Ladybug, Daddy loves you. I have to go get something situated really quick, but I'll be back. You hear me, Sailor Ann Brown? Daddy will always come back for you," he said, giving one last kiss before leaving.

"Go pack your shit. We are leaving," Roxy said to me before walking back to her room. Once I packed as much as my little seven-year-old arms could pack, we drove for a few hours before stopping in front of a big building. *"Here. Give them this paper,"* she said before shoving me out the car.

I watched her drive away, leaving me in front of an orphanage. That was the last time I saw either parent. By the grace of God, Ever's mother, my mother, adopted me. I changed my name and never looked back.

I tried having Raye find my daddy some years back, but it was as if he never existed.

A lone tear fell from my eye as the memories of my past invaded my mind. Before another tear could fall, Lake had already grabbed me and held me in his arms.

CHAPTER 10

Lake

*H*olding Taylor in my arms, I never thought that she would tell me some fucked up shit like that. Just thinking about it made me want to find her moms and murk that bitch. "You know if your moms still alive?"

"We been took care of her... I mean, like, I just don't care to know about her. I just really wanna know what happened to my father," she said.

I had a feeling that there was still more to Taylor than what she was letting on, but I knew when she was ready, she would tell me. Lifting up her face, I softly brushed the tears from her eyes. Looking at her smooth, caramel skin, I didn't even realize she had a beauty mark by her lips. I kissed her, hoping that she could feel my want and need for her.

I just wanted Taylor to know that I would never leave like her parents; I would be there for her even on days when she ain't want me to be. The way I was feeling on her body, I already knew we were about to be in for another fuck session, but before my dick could get fully hard, the consistent ringing of my phone dropped all that.

Answering my phone, I listened as the person on the other end told me some shit that made me want find her evil ass momma and set fire to that hoe. "What the fuck you mean she ain't come to pick up my daughter! Why the fuck y'all call me two whole hours later! I'm fucking somebody up when I get there!" Hanging up the phone, I headed toward my bedroom, quickly throwing on some sweats and a hoodie.

Kim was one crazy ass bitch, fighting bitches, setting my shit on fire, or just being plain ole dumb. But this shit Kim pulled took the cake. This bitch forgot to pick up our fucking daughter from daycare.

"Lake, go 'head and get Ava. I'mma just have my sisters come get me," Taylor said.

I looked at Taylor like she'd just said the fucking stupidest shit ever. "Nah, fuck that. Get dressed. You are coming with me. It's 'bout time you meet Ava anyway. Then I'm taking my two shawties shopping." Coming up behind her as she put back on her heels, I kissed her neck lightly before we headed out to get my baby.

CHAPTER 11

Benny

I walked into the dungeon, another one of our warehouses in the Hunts Points section of the Bronx, and water leaked from the ceiling above. This warehouse wasn't used for our usual business transactions, but if we had meetings here, just know shit wasn't gravy. As I looked into the dark eyes of twelve of my foot soldiers, my eyes landed on this snake motherfucker.

"Benny, man... I... I... I ain't do none of that shit they are saying," Dylan's snake ass said as the blood continued to leak from his mouth, and his eyes were practically swollen shut.

You would think in the two years Dylan had worked for me, he would know not to fucking steal from me.

"Really? So you are calling Tru and Lake liars then?"

Tru and Lake both stared at his punk ass, wishing he would lie on them. I didn't have a doubt in my mind that when my bros told me about Dylan's treason, whether it was true or not.

"Nah, man, I ain't saying that," he said.

"Yeah, ya bitch ass better not be. 'Cause you gonna have to worry about more than Benny if you did, bitch ass nigga," Tru said, coming up and punching the shit out of Dylan in his face.

"Man, my mom needed surgery! I swear I was going to put it back, B," Dylan begged.

"Nigga, do you think I give a fuck about any of that! Your ass just bought a new Benz, but even if you did need it, you knew I would've helped your snake ass!" I yelled at him.

Fuck all that begging he was doing. Fuck the baby he just had that was gonna grow up fatherless, and fuck his mama that was gonna have to bury his ass. Why the fuck should I care about them when he ain't give two fucks about my people?

Taking a look at my tool table that was behind Dylan, I took a deep breath, thinking of what was to come. My eyes landed on the power drill, and a wicked grinned spreader across my face.

"Nah, man! Nooo, please!" he tried to beg as I slowly approach him. Like a lion to his prey, I took the drill to Dylan's left eye, completely drilling straight through his eyeball.

"Yo, hold this nigga down!" I yelled at my two soldiers standing near him, and I drilled his right eyeball as they held him down. His fucking screaming started to piss me the fuck off, so I silenced him with two to the dome.

"Let this be a lesson to all you niggas. I will come for you and everything you fucking love if you cross me. Disloyalty will not be tolerated! Now go clean this shit up, and get eyes on this nigga's mama," I ordered before walking into the backroom to change clothes.

"Your crazy ass just loves using the drill, huh?" Tru asked as we made our way to the parking lot in the back of the dungeon.

All three of us drove our G-Wagons, and no, we didn't plan it either. Fuck you thought this was?

"What can I say? I been told I'm a crazy motherfucker," I responded.

"Yo, y'all wanna roll with me over to Tay Baby house? We gonna play spades and shit. Her sisters gonna be there," Lake said.

All I had planned for the rest of the night was linking up with some thot from Harlem.

"I'm down, but if that pretty one with the big ass fro say some slick shit, I'mma deck her," I warned, hopping in my car.

"Shit, her fine ass sister can braid my hair, and then I'll lay the dick on her ass," Tru's dumbass said before closing his door. We all pulled out of the parking lot.

CHAPTER 12

Ever

"Give me my grandbaby." Grandma Tootie came up and took a giggling Ava from Taylor's arms. For the past month, Taylor had been spending more and more time with Lake. Grandma Tootie basically adopted Ava at that point. Never in a million years would I have thought Taylor would get serious with a nigga. She was the type to fuck 'em and leave—not in a bad way, but that had just always been her style. Well, until now.

"Damn, she looks just like her daddy," Raye said, kissing Ava all over her face, causing her to giggle. We were all in the kitchen, cooking and just chilling. We had a job coming up in a few days, and I liked to unwind before work.

"Who you are telling? I keep telling Lake he gotta have some white in him with his golden hair," Taylor said, running her fingers through Ava's golden curls.

"I hope you have all y'all shit together for this job we got coming up. We don't need any distractions," I said. Looking out for my sisters was just something that came naturally to me. Let them tell it, I was overbearing and boring.

"Relax, Ever! We ain't amateurs! We are going to be ready; no need to be a bitch," Taylor said.

"Well, I wouldn't have to be one if you weren't busy playing house, and this one over here going to every fucking party! We have a business to run, and it seems like I'm the only one who knows that!" I yelled.

"No, you're not. But we wanna have lives too, Ever," Raye chimed in.

"Forget her, Taylor. She ain't been the same since Devin. His ass made Ever not able to trust anybody for shit," Raye said from the other side of the kitchen island. I swore time stopped when she said his name. My sisters knew how painful it still was for me to think about Devin.

"Ever Marie Jones, you betta not. There's a baby in here," Grandma Tootie tried to reason with me, but it was too late. With a quickness, I reached in my back pocket for my hunting knife and threw it straight at Raye's head. If she hadn't ducked when she did, she would have surely been missing an eye.

"This bitch almost got my eye!" she shouted. Everyone, even baby Ava, looked at me as if I had lost my fucking mind.

"How could you, Raye? You know how much that still hurts me to the core." I tried but failed at stopping the tears that escaped my eyes.

"Oh, Ever, I'm so sorry, sis. I don't know what I was thinking." Raye came and quickly took me into a hug, and Taylor joined in.

"I know. It's just some days, it still gets to me."

Wiping my tears, Raye smiled at me. "Well shit, you ain't only gonna be mad at me. Taylor invited them niggas over from the courts," Raye's snitching ass said.

"Raye, you ain't shit." Taylor smirked before walking quickly out of the kitchen. I followed her to the living room where we had set up the spaded table, but before I could say anything to her, the doorbell rang.

CHAPTER 13

Raye

*H*ey, call it what you want, but we were a team, so if I was going down, Taylor's hippie ass was coming with me. I already knew the guys were coming over, and for some reason, I was excited to see Tru's sexy ass again.

Lake's handsome self came through in his all-gray Adidas suit and greeted us before tonguing down Taylor. Benny's brown-skinned, beautiful ass swagged his way in next with his all-white V-neck T-shirt and some black Philipp Plein jeans.

"Wassup, ma?" Tru walked up to me, and his YSL cologne invaded my nose. He looked dumb good in his all-black fit with some white Raf Simons on his feet, and he had his hair in a bun.

"Alright, me and my grandbaby going upstairs. And Ever, baby, loosen up. Give that good-looking boy some play. Show him the trick I taught you with ya tongue," Grandma Tootie said before kissing my sisters and me goodnight and taking Ava with her upstairs.

"What trick with the tongue she is talking about?" Benny smirked at Ever. They were both sitting next to each other.

"Wouldn't you like to know, nigga?" Ever asked. We decided to do

33

teams, and supposedly, Tru said he was good in spades, so this should be an easy win.

Two hours later...

"You a damn liar, Tru!" I said, playfully shoving him. I was over this game. This nigga wasn't even OK at playing spades, and after losing twice, I was done. Surprisingly, Ever and Benny were winning and seemed to really be enjoying each other.

"I'm sorry, Ray Ray. Shit, I'm too fucked up to even think." He sat in between my legs as I took his silky hair down from its bun. The guys had just finished off the last of the Henny, and Taylor had just rolled up another blunt. To say we were lit would be an understatement. Usually, before a job, I liked to just relax, but I was really enjoying hanging out with my sisters and just having good laughs. In the line of business we were in, there wasn't much time for fun.

"What you over there thinking about?" Tru lifted his head back as I looked down into his glossy eyes. As I bit down on my lip, nasty thoughts just came to mind. I didn't know if it was the liquor or me just wanting him.

"Nothing. You wanna go to my room?" I asked, lifting his head back again to stare into his eyes.

"Come here," he said.

I leaned in as our lips connected. I could taste the Henny all over his soft, juicy lips. Damn, this nigga had me weak. Standing up, he reached for my hand as we left everyone else in the living room.

CHAPTER 14

Benny

"Eww, where y'all going?" Ever's nosey ass asked as Tru and Raye made their way upstairs. Who knew that passing up on diving in some of my regular pussy would be worth it?

Ever and I didn't hit it off the first time we met, but after beating everybody's ass with her, I realize she wasn't so bad. From just the short time hanging out with her, I could tell she was guarded and overprotective as fuck over her sisters, but underneath that was a funny, corny, and beautiful ass woman.

"We about to be right behind y'all. Grandma Tottie basically kidnapped Ava from me," Lake said to Taylor as he smacked her ass as she sat on his lap.

"Yeah, she loves that little girl. Shit, we all do, so sorry to say it, Lake, but you stuck with us," she said to him.

"I don't mind, Tay Baby. Plus, I love your grandma; her ass freaky as hell, but I still love her for the way she loves my daughter," Lake said.

If it was one thing you needed to know about Lake, it was that Ava was his weakness. We didn't have much family besides my aunt Dora, who raised Tru and me after we left foster care.

"Alright, B, I'm about to go beat Tay pussy up really quick. Hit me in the a.m." He came and dapped me up before swinging Taylor over his shoulders and carrying her upstairs.

I was so used to females throwing themselves at me, but Ever ass was completely different. Shit, I wasn't too sure if she was even feeling a nigga. She seemed really good at hiding her true emotions.

"So I'm about to head out of here, little momma." I faked staggered to the door. Granted, we did finish off a few bottles of Henny, but I was a pro when it came to holding my liquor.

"Wait, Benny, no. You're drunk. I'm not about to let you drive. Come on," she said, grabbing me by the hand. She turned off the living room lights before heading upstairs. She stopped in front of a door that I assumed was her bedroom, but then she turned around and headed toward another door. Opening up the door that led to her simple but girly ass bedroom, she lightly closed her door. I sat down on her bed.

"Eww, nigga, you better get off my bed with your clothes on!" she barked at me.

"Damn, Ever, if you wanted to see the dick, that's all you had to say," I said.

"Your ass better not pull out your dick, or I'mma fuck you up. I ain't one of your hoes," Ever said, looking dead ass serious.

Pulling my shirt over my head, I threw it on her floor before stepping out of my jeans, only leaving me in my Fendi boxers.

CHAPTER 15

Ever

hy the fuck did he have to look so good? Damn. It'd been so long since a guy had even held my attention, let alone been inside of my bedroom. I had every intention of putting his ass in the guest bedroom, but for some reason, I didn't want to.

Now my ass was stuck on stupid while staring at his tatted chest. "Like what you see?" he asked, licking his lips as if he'd just seen something so delicious. If only he knew that my kitty tasted just that.

"Boy, please. You cute or whatever, but stay on your side," I warned him.

"Why your mama named you Ever?" he asked from behind me, and I turned over to face him. I had lit some of my favorite candles from Bath & Body Works. The candlelight gave me a view of his clear, brown skin. I notice that just above his left eye was a light scar, and for some reason, it added to his sexiness.

"My name is Forever. My parents had trouble having kids. And when my mom finally got pregnant with me, she said she dreamed about me for forever," I told him. "Why your mama named you Benny?" I asked him back.

"She named me after her father, Benjamin, who died before she had me. Why you so closed off?" he shot off another question.

"Uhhh… I hate talking about myself."

It was true. Our father had instilled in us a long time ago to trust no one but family. Everyone else was to be viewed as a potential enemy. I let my guard down once with Devin, and that almost got me killed.

"Man, alright. Your ass will tell me eventually. I bet you that," he said before pulling me into his bare chest.

"Benny?" I softly called his name.

"Huh, sleepyhead?" his raspy voice filled my ear.

"I know your ass wasn't drunk. But I ain't want you to leave."

"Neither did I, Forever." And with that, he kissed the back of my neck, and sleep invaded me.

One Week Later… Business in Vegas

"Damn, shawty, I'm boring you?" our latest target asked as I sent Speeder a quick text before putting my phone back in my YSL purse.

"Not even, baby. It's kind of loud in here. I'm ready to head up." We were inside of the Venetian Hotel. It was a luxury hotel located on the strip in Vegas. My sisters and I had stayed a few times in their penthouse suites. Under different circumstances, we would have stayed a few nights and hit up some clubs… but work called.

"Shit, shawty, I been ready." He rose his hand to signal for the waitress to fetch the check. We made our way to the twenty-sixth floor, and he used his keycard that opened his room door.

"Here. You sit down. I'll make you a drink," I ordered him.

"Give me a kiss first. You so damn pretty, with your big ass fro. I thought I didn't like that whole natural hair shit, but you pull it off well," he said.

Walking over to the sofa where he sat and sitting down on his lap, I gently stroked his face. If the cards had played out differently, I might have actually given him a chance. He reminded me a little of T.I., and after kissing his lips a few times, I made us both a drink.

"So Nova, how a beautiful girl like you ended up in Sin City?" Paul, my mark, asked me as he sipped his whiskey.

"Oh, I run my own business. Just out here to take care of loose ends, then back home," I answered.

"An independent woman—I like that. Shit, I gotta piss. When I come back, I want your ass naked." I watched him close the bathroom door.

Pulling out my phone, I sent Speeder and Keyz another quick text. "Five, four, three, two, o—" Paul came rushing out of the bathroom, holding his throat. He began coughing uncontrollably. He tried to reach for my hand, but I pulled it away. Standing over him, I squatted down so that we were face to face.

"Shhh. Baby, my lip gloss may be a little too popping for you." I wiped off the rest of the poison on my lips. Taking off my gold pendant that held the antidote, I drunk it before screwing it back on.

"Fuck you, bitch! Do you not know who the fuck I am! You're dead! You hear me!" he yelled at me. He had started to vomit up blood; the arsenic mix had begun to take its effect on him.

"No, motherfucker, you are. You don't know who the fuck I am. And since I'm in a good mood, I'll let you in on a secret. I'm your worst fucking nightmare. They don't call me 'Crazy Pistols' for nothing." As soon as my street name left my mouth, it was if this nigga had really already died.

From the moment my sisters and I had come into reign, our identities had to be a secret to those not amongst our organization. We wanted to be respected and felt that if some of our clients knew that three girls ran one of the most powerful assassin organizations in America, they wouldn't take too well to that. There were times when people would talk about Crazy Pistols, Keyz, and Speeder being these savage ass big niggas who did all types of crazy shit to people. But in actuality, we were some pretty girls that took care of their sick grandma, and it just so happened we were very deadly.

"Nah, man, that can't be. The leaders of the Black Skull ain't no bitch. So suck my dick, you—"

One thing I hated was disrespect, especially from a nigga. Pulling his tongue out as far as it could go, I sliced that shit the fuck off. I flung his tongue across the room. He began to holler and cry in pain, as blood started to pour out his mouth.

"Now, where was I before you called me out my name? Yes, I'm *Crazy Pistol*. I know the name doesn't fit such a cute girl like me. Oh yeah, so I guess you already know what's next... Oh my God, shut the fuck up!"

His yelling was really pissing me off, so I pulled out my Glock Gen 5. This shit wasn't even out yet. I shot three rounds in his dick and one in his head. He fucked up the whole speech I had planned for him, but oh well. He saved me some time.

I guess you could say "Crazy Pistols" did fit me because I just loved guns; they were so powerful and deadly—like me. Taylor got her name, Speeder, because she just loved to go fast as hell in any car she had. And they called Raye "Keyz" because you could always hear the tapping of her computer keys as she brought down another mark's cybersecurity system.

Opening the room door, my housekeeping staff entered to begin the cleanup process. Walking to the elevator, I knew Keyz was already at work, deleting any trace of me on the hotel surveillance system.

CHAPTER 16

Taylor

C.P.: Done

After reading the text from Ever, I was ready to get the fuck outta there. Just as I was about to take off my valet vest, some fat, old white man that looked like he could be fucking Santa Clause threw me his car keys. I was able to catch them before they slipped out of my hands.

"Hey, I better not see no fucking scratches on my car," Santa said as he turned to walk away.

"Fuck you, fat ass. This is a 2006 BMW 3-series; this shit already fucked up," I said. Before his fat ass could reply, I pulled off in his car. Hitting 120 miles per hour in Santa Clause's whip, I almost missed my exit. Parking Santa Clause's car in a parking garage a few ways from the hotel, I slit all four of his tires before hopping out.

"Ugh, now I'mma have to burn some sage to cleanse my aura. Fucking dickhead." Like I said before, I was the chill one, but every once in a while, some motherfucker tested your gangster. The old me would have just run his ass over and over again until his fat ass was flat as a pancake.

Finding the mark's car, I slid into the driver's side and drove off. I already had an area in mind as to where I would get rid of the car. When it was all said and done, no traces of him or us being here would exist. This shit was just another day at the office.

Back to NY...

Reclining the seat in our G6 private jet, I pulled out my iPhone to text Lake. Just a few days apart had me missing him bad. I had to make up a lie as to why I wouldn't be in town, and I just felt like shit about it. Lake had always been honest with me about his baby mama, his daughter, and about what he did out in the streets. Lake's name flashed across my screen; he'd beat me to the punch and called me.

"Tay Baby, when you coming back? Have a nigga out here all missing you like I'm Case or some shit," he said.

"Aww, babe, I'm on my flight back now. I miss my Lake and Ava pooh." Just thinking about them brought me peace.

For so long, a commitment was something I was afraid of, but something about Lake—no, something about his soul made me want to give it a try.

"Yeah, man. Shit, I miss Ava too. Grandma Tootie be hogging my baby. But how is ya moms and shit?" he asked me.

"Oh... umm, my mom, yeah, you know she fine now. Lake, I'mma call you when I land," I said, trying to hurry him off the phone.

"You better, Tay... Love you."

Before I could even digest what he said, he hung up. "Lake just told me he loves me." I looked at my sisters, who sat across from me.

"Aww, Taylor finally found the nigga of her dreams," Raye's silly ass said as she came up and hugged me. Ever was quiet, in deep thought.

"What, Ever? Go 'head and say it," I said.

"Taylor, it's only been a few months. We don't know these niggas like that. I need you to stop fucking lighting sage, 'cause it's clouding your judgment", she hissed.

"No, Ever, I see perfectly clear. This is the first time that I ever felt ready for love. Ever, I love him. I love his daughter. I'm finally ready, Ever. I promise to not put our business in jeopardy. But please be happy for me, sister." I didn't know why, but tears started to fall from my eyes. It could've been that I had finally admitted out loud that I was ready for love and all that it'd bring.

"I'm your sister. I will always support you, even if I don't agree with it. So if he makes you happy, then, Tay Tay, go be happy." As she stroked my hand we each held each other's hands like they did in those cheesy movies.

CHAPTER 17

Raye

"So, I guess you don't want to know the 4-1-1 I got on them."
Breaking from the hug and reaching in my Chanel purse, I
handed each of my sisters a folder. Each folder contained all information we would need to know about Tru, Lake, and Benny.

"I had Ricky do some digging for us on them. He said there's some
interesting shit in here." Taylor looked as if she was uncertain about
wanting to know, while Ever just sat there, once again, in deep
thought.

"Nope. I'm good. For once, I'mma just let things play out. If there's
anything Lake wants me to know, he'll tell me," Taylor said, pushing
the folder back toward me.

"Yeah, I agree. Me and Tru are still feeling each other out. I don't
want to stop that 'cause of something in the past. I at least want to get
to know him," I agreed. Ever had her *oh no you bitches didn't* face.

"OK, fine, then we won't look, even though it could be useful.
These niggas could be deadly or some shit," Ever said.

"Oh, please. Who the fuck is deadlier than us?" I wasn't one to
brag, but if y'all hadn't caught it by now, we were some bad bitches.

We were the leaders of the most notorious underground assassin origination in America, and we went by the Black Skull.

"Ever, no one is deadlier than the Black Skull. Plus, I think your ass just wanna make sure Benny ain't crazy or nothing. 'Cause your ass like him," Taylor teased Ever, who blushed in embarrassment.

"Fuck y'all," she said, flipping us both off.

A Few Days Later...

"Oh shit, Tru, I'm cumming!" I moaned, cumming hard all over his dick. A few more strokes later, Tru was right behind me. Kissing his soft lips, I gently pulled on the braids I put in his head last night.

"Get that ass in the shower. I wanna take you out," he said, smacking my ass. I watched his naked, strong, sexy body roll out of bed as he walked toward his bathroom.

"Yes, we about to turn up. Where we are going? 40/40? Sin?" I asked.

"No, turn-up queen. Just shut up and get dressed," he said.

I hated not knowing where I was going. How the fuck would I know if I should wear heels, flats, or panties? Shit.

Thinking about it, I'd never really been on a date. I had boyfriends in the past, but I never pushed for anything more than what they gave. So, if a nigga wanted to Netflix and fuck all day, I was with it. Tru wanting to get to spend time with me outside of the bedroom was something new to me.

After finally washing up and settling for an all-black Fashion Nova jumpsuit and my Balenciaga sneakers, I was ready to go.

"About damn time, Ray Ray. Your ass took like two hours," he said.

"Nigga, don't act like I wasn't sucking your dick in the shower, and you ate my pussy after I got out the shower," I told him.

"Yeah, yeah, shut up and come on, big head." He locked up his house, and I walked behind him, just admiring his sexy ass. He had on a white shirt with "Vale Boys" written in red across it. He paired it with some white shorts and white Ones, and this nigga had on the most blinged-out ankle bracelet I'd ever seen.

"Stop looking at my dick, and get in the car, Ray Ray." Sliding into his Bentley, we pulled off.

"Why you call me Ray Ray?" I asked him. He barely ever called me by my name, and I thought it was so cute that he had a special nick-name just for me.

"'Cause Raye sound like a nigga's name, and plus, I just can, nigga." He smirked, showing his lower bottom grill.

"Anybody ever told you that you look like Ryan from *Black Ink Chicago?*" I asked him.

Don't get me wrong. Tru had his own sexiness about him, but if you were to put him and Ryan in the same room, you would think they were twins. I rubbed my hands over his head. Touching or playing with his hair was something I found myself often doing. It could be that his hair was just so nice to touch or that a bitch was secretly jealous that this nigga had the prettiest hair ever.

"Nah, but they do say that I look like Tru from Brooklyn." His smart mouth was something I would have to get used to, but I wasn't complaining.

CHAPTER 18

Benny

"Laser tag? Tru, since when does your ass take any bitch anywhere?" I asked him.

I knew Tru my whole life, and I'd never even seen him take a bitch to a doctor's appointment, let alone a date. So to sit there and listen to this nigga tell us about his date with Raye was something new, but it wasn't surprising. Out of all of us, Tru was low-key the romantic type. Lake's ass was the ready to settle-down ass type, and me, I was the take my time ass type 'cause if a girl tried to play me, I'd shoot her ass.

"Man, never, but I just want shawty to know that it's more than about the pussy... even though that shit A-1," he said.

"And she beat me. Like Ray Ray really good at shooting. That girl could be a sniper," he said while I shook my head at these niggas just out here on some sucker shit.

"Man, I gotta stay away from y'all soft ass niggas. This one basically married now. I called this nigga phone, and Taylor picks up," I said, pointing at Lake.

"Fuck you, nigga. Ain't shit soft over here." Before I could get into Lake's ass, FatBoy came running up to us.

We didn't call this nigga FatBoy for nothing. He had to be about at least a solid 450 pounds, and out of the five years I'd know this nigga, this was the first time I ever saw him run. FatBoy stood before us, barely able to talk. I made sure to step back a little 'cause he looked like he was about to pass out, and my ass sure wasn't gonna catch him.

"Nigga, breathe. You know your ass can't run for more than a second," Tru said, causing FatBoy to inhale and exhale quickly

"So-some... Some nigga just ran up in Aunt D crib." That was all that needed to be said as my brothers and I hopped in my whip and sped toward my aunt's house. My aunt Dora was the strongest woman I know.

When my mother died, and my pops want to jail, I got sent to a group home. I lived in that group home for almost two years, and that's where I met Tru. My aunt was a crack addict but went to rehab and got her degree, and when she got a crib, she came for me, and she even took Tru.

"Aunt D!" As I looked around the house we bought her, everything looked ransacked.

"Benny, I'm in here!"

Walking into the kitchen, I found her sitting at the dining room table with her hand on head. Lifting her head up, you could see the dried-up tears and blood.

"On everything I love, niggas is dying for this shit!" Tru slammed his fist into the wall.

"Tru, baby, I'm OK. Just give thanks to God for that," she said.

"No, Aunty, tell us what happened," Lake said, taking a seat by her.

"One minute, I'm in the kitchen, cooking, and the next, these two-big motherfuckers come in. They kept asking for money, and when I told them I didn't have it, they beat me up and messed up the house. I think the only reason they stopped was because they saw y'all pictures I have hanging up," she told us.

"Yeah, 'cause them niggas know they done fucked up." To say we were pissed would be too light.

Aunt D was the glue to what family we had left, and these niggas didn't know that they just signed their own death certificates.

"Come on, Aunt D. You can stay with me until we get this shit figured out," Lake said, helping her up.

"Lake, I will still pop you in the mouth for cussing like that. OK, let me go get my bible at least. Can't wait to see my baby Ava and this girl Benny and Tru done told me about." One thing about Aunt D was she couldn't keep a secret to save her life.

We only told her about that so she could cook her famous fried chicken for us; if I had known her ass was gonna snitch, I wouldn't have... Nah, I would've. Her chicken was lit.

Later That Night...

"I want these niggas A-fucking-SAP," I told all thirty of my most loyal hitters. We had put out the word that if anybody knew the niggas that ran up in our aunt's crib, holla at us.

I felt so disrespected that somebody would have the audacity to even fucking touch my aunt. At that moment, I needed to put two into them niggas' heads and some good pussy 'cause a nigga was stressed.

"Alright, yo, we are heading out. About to go to this double date shit," Lake said. I shook my head. These niggas got softer and softer every fucking day.

"Alright, y'all be safe, bros." After dapping them up, I opened my car door.

"Aye, Benny, if you change your mind, Ever's staying home tonight!" Lake yelled from his car before pulling away. Damn, baby girl had been on my mind lately. We texted and spent hours on the phone a few times after game night, but I could tell she was holding back. I wasn't one to chase any hoe, so I backed off.

Throwing my keys on my kitchen counter, I pulled my Gucci sweater over my head and threw it on my couch. I had purchased this a condo in the city a few years back. I didn't see the need to own a home yet when it was just the countless hoes I had running through here and me. As I walked further into the condo, light R&B music was being played from the back where my bedroom was.

"Yo, I know motherfuckers ain't this fucking stupid." I laughed because there was about to be a fucking bloodbath once I got finished with whoever tried to violate.

"What now, bitch ass n... Alexis!" Looking into the scared eyes of one of the only woman I used to love, I felt nothing. This bitch broke into my house, made herself right at home, and was standing in front of me ass naked... which wasn't that bad.

Lexis and I went way back. I was talking *sneaking out past curfew to fuck* way back. She was the only girl I ever thought about marrying. Something about her just drew me to her. Alexis was the type of female that had nothing to bring to the table but her looks. After I started to make a name for myself and get paper, I gave Alexis $30,000 and told her to invest in herself.

Most bitches would have gone to school, opened up a business, or bought a house. Not Lexis though. She blew that $30,000 in less than a month, and to this day, I couldn't tell you on what. But it didn't matter; I'd always have some type of love for Alexis because we shared something I would treasure forever. A child.

"Yo, bitch, you really out of your fucking mind, thinking you can just come up in my shit unannounced."

"Why I gotta be all that, Benny? I just missed you," she said, slowly walking her naked, smooth, vanilla body toward me, and I couldn't do anything but admire it. I stared at the tattoo on her left arm with my and my daughter's names on it.

She still had that baby weight from our daughter, but it did her good. Her long, black weave was bone straight, and her perky titties sat up just right. Her slanted, green eyes looked full of lust. She stopped right in front of me before getting down on her knees.

As she started to tug at my jeans, as much as I didn't want to, I stopped her. The feelings I had for Lex left me a long time ago. Pushing her lightly off of me, I left her ass laying there and looking stupid on the couch as I went and took a shower.

"What the fuck? Yo, Lexis, get the fuck up and get the fuck out." I came out of the shower, and this bitch was still in the same spot I left her.

"Aww, come on, Benny. When the fuck you gonna stop punishing me?" she asked as tears started to fall from her eyes.

"Come on, man. I don't got time for this shit," I told her.

"No. Benny, I'm tired of you treating me like shit!" Walking up to me, she got in my face and mushed me in my head.

After that, I saw red. I yoked Alexis ass up by her throat and slammed her hard as fuck into my wall.

"You wanna talk! Talk then, Lex! Let's talk about how my fucking daughter died because your ass fell asleep behind the wheel! Let's talk about how she's the only reason you're still alive! Because every time I see your face, I see hers! Fuck you, Lexis!" After slamming her one last time, I grabbed my house keys before walking out. No final warning was needed; I knew for a fact Alexis would be up and out of my shit.

CHAPTER 19

Ever

"$\mathcal{E}$ver, I don't know why you didn't go out with your sisters," Grandma Tottie said to me with a giggling Ava in her arms. Grandma Tottie loved her some Ava. Shoot, we all did. That little girl had us wrapped around her fingers.

"'Cause, Grandma, it's a double date, and I am no one's third wheel. I'm too cute for that," I told her.

"That you are, but, baby, you sit up in this house, wasting your life away. Ever, baby, you gonna have to let go of that pain you have; let happiness take over and love again. Ever, don't be afraid to jump." Her words hit me like a ton of bricks.

Over the last few years, I used my work as a way to distract me from the emptiness I always felt. A sense of darkness was beginning to fill me, and I didn't think I could or wanted to stop it. My family had seen the changes in me, and they tried so desperately to help make me feel better. The world was at my fingertips, yet I chose to not even grab it not even a bit of it. Since Devin, I'd lost myself. My happiness, smile, and wanting love left when he did.

"Grandma, it's so hard," I said as she hugged me. The ringing of the doorbell got my attention. Turning on the hidden security cameras through the TV, I was able to see who was on the other side.

"Why the hell is he here?" I asked myself. As I pulled the door open, there stood Benny, and he was looking just as fine as ever. His pretty, white teeth and deep dimples were the first things I saw. Benny had on this season's Balenciaga men's jean jacket that I had been eyeing for myself with some simple, black jeans, and of course, every nigga just had to rock some type of Jordans. He walked right around me.

"How are you doing, beautiful?" he asked Grandma Tottie, giving her and Ava kisses. He turned his attention to me, and bending down, he gave me a hug, and his Dior Savage cologne invaded my nose. "You ready to go?" his ass asked me after kissing me lightly on the neck.

"Ummm... no. I'm 'bout ready to go to bed," I said confusedly.

"No, she ready to go. Here, Ever, your coat." Grandma Tottie handed me the first coat she saw. Mind you, my hair was in a messy bun, and I was in my Juicy Couture sweatsuit. I had no intentions of going anywhere with anyone. Man, I wished I had put on something cute.

"Grandma, look at me. I'm not even dressed" I whined.

"Oh, shut up, Ever. You look beautiful without even trying. Now, go have fun and maybe even get some loving. See ya in the morning," she said, basically shoving me out the house.

"OK, fine, but you better not try no funny shit. I'll fuck you up, Benny," I told him.

"Yeah, sure. Get in the car, ugly," he said, opening up his car door for me.

Taking in the city view, I couldn't help but steal glances at him. He always seemed so serious but also gentle. My sisters told me about what they knew about him, and he was really out here making a name for themselves. He caught me staring and gave me a wink before quickly looking away. After driving for a few, we ended up on the Westside of the city. He parked his Range in front of a restaurant called Negril.

"Hello, Mr. Carter. We have everything ready," the short Puerto

Rican hostess with the fat ass said. Following her, I noticed that the restaurant was empty besides the staff.

"This place must be trash 'cause ain't no one here," I said.

"Nah, ma. This just how it looks when you buy out the restaurant to impress a mean, little woman with the curly fro." He smiled, showing the deep dimples on his clear, brown skin, and I blushed at his comment.

"How did you even know I would come?" I asked. The host showed us to our table, and Benny pulled out my chair before taking a seat across from me.

"Because I was going to drag your ass here. Ain't gonna have me wasting my money, shit," he said.

"Well, thank you. That's the most thoughtful thing ever," I told him.

"Chill, shawty. Don't go getting soft. I'm trying to fuck." He laughed as the waiter walked up and took our order.

"So you do have a romantic side. Your momma taught you well, Mr. Benny," I said, taking another bite of my food.

"Nah, my aunt raised me. My moms died..." His lips look so juicy as he talked, and I just wanted to bite 'em.

"If you want me to kiss you, Forever, just come and get it," he said in his raspy voice.

Benny stared at me while my stupid ass was stuck. I wanted to do some nasty things to this man, and I didn't know why. It was beyond his physical appearance, which was a plus, but also just his aura. Over dinner, I found out a lot about Benny. He carried himself with so much confidence, and he asked me questions that I never even thought to ask myself. He seemed like the type to want to see the people around him prosper.

"Listen, Ever, I'm low-key feeling you. And the way you keep looking at me like you want me to throw your ass on this table right now and eat your pussy from the back is very tempting right now." Tucking in his lips, he pushed his chair out. I didn't know what came over me, but the next thing I knew, my ass was sitting on his lap.

As I kissed his lips, he slipped his tongue into my mouth. Tugging my sweats down, I made sure to never break our kiss. Grabbing the sides of his face, I bit and sucked on his lower lips. Letting out a low moan, he sucked on my neck, leaving a hickey for sure.

"Nah, E, we can't do it like this."

Fuck that. I needed this. Grandma Tottie said to jump—well, shit, I was leaping.

"Please, Benny, I need this. Make me feel good," I said, nodding my head yes.

"Your dinner will be out shortly," our waiter said with our drinks in hand.

"Fuck the dinner. And if your ass come back, I'mma fuck you up," he said, threatening the waiter. The poor waiter basically ran out, and once again, we were left alone.

Throwing everything off the table, he gently placed me on my back. Then he sat down in the chair with my legs open, and he ate my pussy like no other. With his mouth on my clit, he pulled my breasts out of my shirt and began to play with my already hard nipples. You could see my juices dripping from his mouth.

"Damn, E, your shit taste so sweet," he said, licking each of his fingers clean of my juices. After he dropped his jeans and freed his dick, I had second thoughts. The width and the length of his dick had me wondering if he would even fit in me.

"Wait, Benny. I haven't done this in a while. Be gentle," I said.

"I got you. I don't know what it is about you, Forever, but I want to always see you happy." After I nodded my head, he kissed me so passionately that I got wet all over again.

Who would have thought that Benny, the nigga I thought about putting a bullet in, would end my celibacy?

"Damn, E, your shit tight as fuck," he hissed in his raspy voice.

When he was finally able to enter me fully, he slowly stroked in and out of me. My pussy soaked his dick. I'd never felt this much ecstasy. After a few more strokes of him hitting my spot, I squirted all on the dick, and he came soon after.

"Here. Let me wipe you up. I'mma just have them pack up the food, and we can eat at my place," he ordered as he finished cleaning me up with the napkins on our table.

CHAPTER 20

Raye

"Look who it is trying to creep in here after being gone for two days," I said, looking at Ever's sneaky ass creep home.

She looked different; she looked happy, something I hadn't seen my sissy look in a long time. Her loss of happiness didn't only affect her but us as a family. Things like partying, girl time, or just talking to one another were few and far between. Business became more important to her rather than her family, but I knew it was all coming from a place of hurt. So to see my sister just smiling at nothing and looking crazy was nice.

"Oh shit, she done got some dick. Spill it, Ever. I already tracked your location at Benny's condo," I told her.

A grin spread across her face like her nasty ass was remembering all the nasty stuff she did last night.

"OK... Bitch, I got the dick, and damn, it was bomb. Had me wanting to change my ways and settle down. Plus, he's really sweet— an asshole but sweet." She tried to bypass us, but Taylor and I were right on her.

I flopped down on Ever's bed. "What happened to the clothes you left out in? Benny tore them shits off, huh?" I asked her as she stepped out of her new ripped jeans and a simple tan top with this season's new Gucci bag.

"Y'all, we fucked on the restaurant table," she blurted out.

"Oh damn, that shit sounds surprisingly sexy," Taylor chimed in as she texted on her phone.

"And then we want back to his house and literally sat up just talking. He had a fucked-up childhood, but somehow, this nigga became the king of New York. Did you know that besides the basketball tournaments, they host talent shows and block parties for the kids?" she asked.

Tru had already told me about all the good they did within the community, but he also told me how he felt torn in between the two. Because on the one hand, he wanted to be the positive role model for kids, but the next, he was pushing poison into the same community he was trying to help.

"Yeah. Lake said their talent shows be lit. We might have to audition 'cause y'all know I can sing," Taylor's lying ass said.

"So, I take it you told him that your one of the ruthless leaders of the infamous Black Skull?" I asked her.

"Yeah right. So I'm just supposed to say, 'oh yeah, Benny, I'm a trained assassin and a billionaire.' Nah, I'll pass." Ever could be so stubborn at times, but I understood where she was coming from.

We vowed a long time ago to never reveal ourselves to those that weren't a part of our organization, but we never said anything about when we opened ourselves to love.

"Alright, y'all, I gotta a get ready to meet up with Tru. I'm taking him to a shooting range," I said, getting up from the bed.

"Raye, what you need to be doing is ending shit with Red before going any further with Tru." Leave it to Ever to bring up Red.

See, Red was this well-known Blood nigga from the A that I kind of was in a relationship with. We had been together for two years. Our relationship wasn't much to brag about, because all we mostly did was sit up in his crib and fuck. When I came up to New York and started messing with Tru, it was like *Red who?*

"Ever, ain't nobody worried about no got damn Red. Hello?" I answered my phone, listening to our most trustworthy hitter, Ricky, relay some information to me, and I became livid. "OK, Ricky, I want all eyes on her, and I need these niggas' names in the next hour!" I hung up without any more words needed to be said.

"The guys' aunt got robbed last night. That's why Tru just canceled on my ass. I was about to hack his fucking phone and erase all his shit," I said.

"What!" Taylor damn neared jumped out her skin. It was kind of nice to see calm Taylor react. It took a lot to get a reaction out of Taylor, so to see her care about someone other than family was different.

"Don't worry. I put eyes on her, and—" My phone rang again with Ricky on the other end. After listening to what he had to say, I hung up. "Let's go. He found them niggas already." Changing into our classic all-black attire, we walked to Grandma's attic that held all our weapons. Taylor grabbed her Beretta, I grabbed my Glock, while Ever went for her AK-47. Taylor and I shared a glance with each other, probably both thinking the same thing.

"Damn, Ever! You can't tell me you don't love that nigga," Taylor said.

CHAPTER 21

Lake

$\mathcal{W}$e finally got word on the niggas that ran up in Aunt D's crib. I sat in the back of the unmarked car we got, and Benny and Tru sat in the front. We had been sitting in this car for about a good hour, waiting for these niggas. Aunt Dora was back at my house with Ava while we were handling these niggas.

"Man, so these niggas came all the way from D.C. just to rob a random lady's house?" Tru asked as he passed the blunt to Benny.

"From what Fatboy told me, these niggas just been going around town and fucking robbing people. I guess that's why their dumb asses ain't know Aunt D was off limits." Benny put his attention back on the house where these niggas were supposed to be.

"Man, Tay Baby, hit me back when you get this shit, B," I said, hanging up my phone. This was the third time I called her ass, and she didn't pick up. It wasn't like Tay Baby; we literally kept in contact all day, and she usually answered whenever I called.

"Man, Ray Ray ass ain't picking up either. All I know is her ass betta not be in no nigga's face," Tru said.

"Shit, E ain't hit me back all day either. After this, I'm heading over there to put some respect on my name," Benny said. We were all over here worried about our girls instead of focusing on lighting these niggas up.

"Man, where these motherfuckers at? Oh shit, I see a car pulling up," Benny said.

We all watched as the two big ass niggas that ran up in our aunt's crib exited out of a beat-up Honda. They were laughing and smiling like shit was just gravy.

Doublechecking to make sure my nine was on me, I reached for the car handle. "Yo, Lake, hold up. Another car is coming," Benny said as he grabbed my arm before I could open the car door.

"Get down," Tru said as some all-black unmarked car cruised past us and stopped right in front of the two niggas. We couldn't hear what was being said, but we saw the two niggas stop and look at the car. Suddenly, the car doors flew open, and three figures rushed out with precision. They circled around them in seconds. One of the unknown niggas had a big ass AK-47.

"What the fuck is going on?" Benny asked more to himself, but I was pretty sure Tru and I were thinking the same thing. The lights and sounds of gunfire could be seen as they riddled those niggas with bullets.

"Yo, they just lit those niggas up like the Fourth of July!" Tru said, surprised.

"Fuck that! Them niggas moved like a fucking swat team!" I yelled because I couldn't believe the shit that was happening in front of my face. It was like a scene out of a hood book... Nah, this shit was some movie type shit.

One of the unknown killers kneeled onto the bodies of the niggas we were gonna kill. After doing whatever it was he was doing, they started to walk back to their car. But suddenly, one of them pointed in our direction.

"Oh shit! I think they see us," Benny said as all three killers stopped and faced us with their guns drawn.

At this time, my bros and I already had our shit in our hands, ready to bust some shots. But for some reason, they just left. Shit, they were lucky 'cause we wouldn't have been such an easy kill.

After the killers pulled off, we got out and walked toward the niggas that we came for. Thank God we were in the hood, so no cops were coming anytime soon.

"Damn, these niggas had beef with the Black Skull," I said. Looking at the riddled bodies of these snake niggas, I saw each of their foreheads had *B.S.* carved into them—a signature of a Black Skull kills. I couldn't help but wonder how they got into it with the Black Skull.

"Man, fuck the Black Skull! If I had known it was them niggas, I would have blasted their asses!" Benny yelled as he let out shots into the already dead bodies before walking away.

"Man, this shit is too much, bro. I need some head," Tru said before giving one last look at the dead niggas on the ground and walking away.

As I turned to walk away, I heard the sound of coughing. "Please help me," this weak motherfucker said as blood poured out of his mouth. "Fuck you, nigga. See you in hell." With that, I let off rounds into his head.

CHAPTER 22

Taylor

After we dumped the car I stole, we were home in no time. We didn't usually make spontaneous kills, and it had me on edge after seeing the guys there tonight. Never had we gotten so close to being exposed, and I wasn't too sure if we weren't.

"Shit, I hope they ain't see too much," Ever said as we walked into her bedroom. We had already changed and showered.

"I was about to light their asses up. Thank God Ever peeped it was them," Raye said as we all sat around Ever's bed.

"Girls, y'all little boyfriends downstairs." Grandma Tottie came in with Ava on her hip. Taking my baby girl out her hands, we made our way downstairs. Seeing the guys standing in the living room with the meanest faces ever, I just knew that our cover had been blown.

They each stood there expressionless, making it hard to know what they were thinking. Even with his blank stare, Lake was the most handsome man I had ever seen.

His fit was really simple like always—all-black everything. He finally listened to me and put up his golden locks into those cute, messy top-knot buns. Joining him at the bottom of the stairs, I embraced him in a hug before kissing him.

"Lake, I can explain. See, we are—" I tried to quickly explain.

"Hell yeah, your ass better explains why you ain't pick up my calls." He huffed as he took Ava out my arm and kissed her and me.

My sisters and I all shared a look of relief, and they probably would've gotten in my ass later for getting ready to snitch. Here I was, thinking Lake and the guys figured out who we were, but all my babe was worried about was why I didn't answer my phone. Each day, this man made me happy that I finally decided on him.

"Yeah, Ray Ray, your ass better not been in no nigga's face," Tru said before grabbing a handful of Raye's ass and giving her a sloppy kiss.

"Come on, Forever," Benny called to Ever with his hand out. To my surprise, she kissed us goodbye and took his hand then left.

Raye and I shared a smirk. "Come on, Tay Baby," Lake said with a sleeping Ava in his arm. Tru and Raye left out with us, and after kissing my sister goodbye, we went our separate ways.

After tucking Ava into bed, I did some light meditation while Lake showered. I meditate daily because it helped me become self-aware and less stressed. The Taylor you knew wasn't always this way.

I was in really dark places mentally, mostly because of my past regarding my family. There were times where I took extra missions without my sisters just so I had the chance to kill more. But after discovering yoga, my chakra, and meditation, I had been in a better head space.

"So how was your day?" I asked Lake after lighting some candles and putting on Sade's smooth voice. He had just come from out the shower, shirtless, in his Calvin Klein boxers. His locs were a little damp as they hung loosely, landing at the middle of his back. One of the most attractive things to me about Lake was that this man had not one scar, scratch, or tattoo on his body; he was perfect.

After handing him an ecstasy pill, we both washed them down with some water. Lake and I usually popped pills or rolled a blunt together, and the sex we had when we were high was unexplainable.

Before y'all go thinking we were some drug addicts, it was something we did not do often and only when Ava was asleep or away.

"Shit was crazy. But I don't want to think about that. I got your beautiful ass in my bed," he said while rolling on top of me and spreading my legs open. Kissing my lips intensely, he already had me about to explode, and I wasn't even feeling my pill yet.

"Damn, this kitty stays wet for daddy, huh?" he asked as he pulled his fingers out of me. He took control, and his pillow-soft lips devoured my kitty. Trying my hardest not to wake Ava, I grabbed his locs into my hands as he killed my pussy.

"Damn, Tay Baby, your shit just gets tighter," he said, kissing my inner thighs and still fingering me.

"Yeah, yoni eggs," I moaned out as he hit my spot with his thick tongue. After a few rounds, we were beyond tired; that mixed with the day's events, sleep was well needed.

A Few Days Later...

"Hi, my pretty girl," I cooed after Ava. I didn't know how, but it became natural for me to step up and take on Ava as my own. Her mother hadn't come around since her dumb ass left her at daycare. I vowed to be a role model for her, and even if Lake and I didn't work out, I would still be there for her.

"Let me get a bite," Raye said as she took a big ass bite of my pizza. My sisters and I decided to have a girls' day out, so we did some shopping at the mall.

"Bitch, you lucky I love you." I faked an attitude.

"You better, hoe. Ever, let me get some iced tea," she said before taking Ever's drink. Ever didn't even notice; she was too focused on her phone. My sister had been smiling more lately, and she just had this beautiful glow to her. My bet was that Benny had the magic touch after all.

"Ain't that Benny right there?" I asked.

"Where!" Ever shot her head up from her phone so quick and started looking all around; I was surprised she didn't crack her neck.

"I knew it! So, are y'all like official now?" I asked her while feeding Ava some fries.

"I don't know. I'm too afraid to ask. We're always together when we don't work, and I'm pretty sure he would fuck a nigga up for even breathing on me." She blushed just from the thought of him.

I never imagined the old Ever would come back—the Ever that smiled, laughed, and wasn't so closed off from us.

"Well, whatever it is, I love it," Raye said as we continued to just browse around the mall.

"Who the fuck is you?" some fake-booty Nicki Minaj wannabe asked. She was thick as hell, and her light skin was caked up in makeup. She was chewing her gum loudly while rolling her eyes at us all at the same time.

"Bitch, I'm me," I said, stepping to her with my sisters right by me. This bitch was so loud that people began to notice and stop. I hated when people brought unwanted attention to me; it made me feel like they were testing my gangster or something.

"This bitch done fucked up today," Raye said in a giggle while taking off her gold, engraved *Tru* hoop earrings. At that point, just by looking at the way my sisters stood, I knew they were ready for some action.

Ever stayed calm, but I knew better. If this girl made the wrong move, there was definitely gonna be a news report later on a grue-some homicide. That was if we were nice enough to leave a body.

"You over there in matching outfits and shit with my daughter like you her fucking momma. Lake got me fucked up!" she yelled, looking at Ava and me in our matching Gucci dresses. Shit, if I were a basic hoe like her, I would be mad too. This bitch tried to take Ava from her stroller, and I nearly lost my mind. I quickly grabbed her by the wrist and didn't let go until I felt and heard a snap.

"Ahhh! I think you broke my wrist! You crazy bitch! I don't want you around *my daughter!*" she yelled out in pain.

Her words resurrected something in me and brought thoughts I tried to suppress for a while. Ava wasn't my daughter, and this selfish thot could take her from me legally if she wanted to. It didn't matter if I was the one who taught her how to count, kissed her boo-boos, or tucked in at night. She belonged to Lake and this sorry excuse for a woman.

My sisters laughed at her dumb ass, but I was beyond pissed. Invading her space as she lay on the floor in pain, I said, "I will fucking kill you for mines. And if you ain't know, Ava and Lake are mines now. So take the broken wrist as a warning. 'Cause, baby, I promise you this here ain't what you want." My sister's and I moved around her as she continued to yell out in pain

"Fuck you recording? My dick in your mouth!" Raye yelled at some random girl who had started to record the incident. Raye grabbed the girls' phone right out of hand, and the girl, I guess, was too afraid to say anything to her.

Mall security came running past us to the bitch on the ground. All you could hear was them calling for backup and her calling us every name but the ones our momma gave us.

"No, leave me the fuck alone, and go get them crazy ass bitches!" she yelled as we exited out of the mall and made our way to Country, our bodyguard, who was waiting for us.

"You know it doesn't matter, right?" Ever asked me as I finished strapping a sleeping Ava into her car seat.

Closing the car door, I asked, "What doesn't?"

"You not being Ava's biological mother. It doesn't matter, because you're ten times of a better mother than that thing back there will ever be, and you ain't even try. Plus, you're Speeder of the Black Skull. You can make anything happen." Calling me by my street name, she winked at me as she climbed into the backseat of the car.

"Oh shit, you're right." And with that, any doubt I had left my mind, and thoughts of Ava being my daughter surfaced.

CHAPTER 23

Red

Raye really had me fucked up if she thought her ass could just skip town on a nigga. Raye and I had been in a relationship for little over two years. When her ass wasn't disappearing for days, and her nosy, bitch ass sisters minded their business, our relationship was great. I met her the weirdest way too.

My nigga Buzz had gotten into some deep shit with the Black Skull. First of all, any nigga alive knew not to fuck with those niggas. Anyway, I met Raye around the neighborhood Buzz was hiding out at. We started to kick it heavy, and one day, I took her with me to drop off some money to Buzz.

While in the house, some masked men came rushing in like fucking ninjas and shit. Long story short, they lit Buzz's ass the fuck up and carved *B.S.* in his forehead. And when they went to go shoot me, Raye stood in front of the gunman, ready to take the bullet for me.

Ever since then, I'd been hooked on her. Any bitch that was willing to die for you was a loyal bitch you needed on your team. Yeah, I did my dirt; so the fuck what? Raye still wasn't supposed to just leave a nigga.

Flicking the last bit of my blunt on the pavement, I watched from my rental as a car pulled up to Raye's grandmother's house. I had remembered her grandmother's address from when we drove up from the A to Brooklyn to check on her old ass.

After watching some big ass, black, gorilla-looking nigga opening the back door of a Cadillac for Raye, I opened my driver side door.

"Hi, Doe, shawty." Catching her by surprise, I couldn't help but get caught in her beauty. She had on a nude crop top, bringing attention to her nipple rings and some ripped-up jeans, and she paired it with the Gucci sneakers I surprised her with. But the most beautiful thing about her would have to be her face and those damn freckles.

"Red! What you doing here? Last I checked, you was in Florida," she said, looking down the street nervously.

"How the fuck you know that?" Before I could even step to her, the gorilla motherfucker blocked me.

"You good, boss?" this nigga asked Raye but never moved from in front of me.

"Boss! Nigga, I'm the fucking boss, and if you don't move your big Wesley Snipes looking ass out my way!" I shoved the shit outta him, and this nigga didn't even budge.

"Country, you know I'm a big girl. Yeah, I'm good," Raye said. Giving me one last look, he walked away.

"Raye, what the fuck? First, you go missing on a nigga, and now, some big nigga checking me?" I asked. But she didn't pay me any mind, turning and walking toward her grandmother's door.

"What, Rashawn? I told you that I came here to take care of my grandma!" she said, closing the front door.

"Yeah, but what does that have to do with us? Huh, Raye? Got me tracking your ass down like I'm some little nigga," Just thinking about how she just disappeared on me had me on a hundred.

"I just had a lot on my mind, and—" Before she could finish, tears fell from her eyes. Seeing her cry made me forget why I was mad in the first place.

"Don't cry, babe. I'm sorry." Kissing her neck, I knew I would get the drawers. Reaching for her pants, she stopped me midway.

"Red, you gotta stop. My grandma is upstairs," she said.

"Listen, I'mma be in the city for a few days. Hit me when you free, Raye." Grabbing her face, I stared into her eyes, and there, all I saw were lies.

Brushing the feelings away because I knew Raye, I gave her one last kiss before sliding to this bitch named Bia's crib that lived in Queens. What? I said I was a boss, right!

CHAPTER 24

Ever

"*R*eally, Raye, you cried?" I literally had tears in my eyes from laughing as my sister told me what had happened to her.

"What, bitch? I ain't know what else to do." She huffed through my phone.

"You could have started by telling that man the truth. That you found someone better, who look better, and treat you better. Raye, Tru ain't nothing like Red's lame ass," I told her. For the life of me, I couldn't figure out why Raye wouldn't just come clean to Red.

"Listen, I don't want to keep you from your dinner with Benny and his aunt. But, Ever, don't give me advice on telling someone the truth when you can't do it either," she said, and before I could even reply, this heffa hung up on me. Checking myself out once more in the mirror, I rejoined Benny and Aunt D at the table.

"Oh, child, thank God you back. I had to hold this boy from coming to get you," Aunt D said to me with a look of relief on her face.

"Man, she ain't hold nothing back. I was just about to go get you. You good, Forever?" he asked me with his brown eyes full of concern.

"Yes, poppa, I just had to freshen up. So, Aunt D, you left off telling me how Benny used to sleep with a teddy bear at ten years old." Dinner with Benny and his aunt was filled with nothing but laughter and a few embarrassing moments for Benny.

It was still early in the day when we dropped Aunt D off from dinner. Over dinner, it was hard not to notice the love she had for all her boys as if she had birthed them herself. Aunt Dora was a strong woman for overcoming years of drug addiction to be there for her nephew. I could tell that Benny really cherished her, and she was the last bit of any form of blood family he had left.

"Ever, beloved, it was so good to meet the girl who tamed the beast," she said to me, giving me one last hug as Benny held open the door for her. I watched from the car window as they interlocked arms and walked up toward her door. They stood there and talked a little while also stealing glances at me. Over the years, I had mastered the skill of reading lips, and as much as my nosy self-wanted to know what they were saying, I let Benny and Aunt Dora have their moment.

"Aunt D says you da one, shawty," he said as I stared at his sexy ass.

He looked so handsome as I stared across in the passage side of his Porsche. Every detail about this man did something to me from his low waves to the word *savage* written right above his right eyebrow, or it could be how just the simplest outfits looked so good on him.

"You are doing it again, Forever," Benny said, grinning, never taking his eyes off the road. "Whattt? I can't help it. Today, I had to tell some nigga that slid in my DM with a dick pic that the only dick I want pictures of is my man's. 'Cause I be on it faithfully." While I rubbed his chin hairs, he reached over for my phone.

"What nigga! See, niggas be wanting to die!" he said.

"Benny, if your crazy ass don't give me my phone back and watch the road." Taking my phone back from him, I noticed that we weren't going toward the way home.

"Where are we going, poppa?" I asked as we pulled into Green-

Wood Cemetery. Stopping the car, he got out and came to open my door.

"Just wanna show you something," he said as his light-brown eyes danced with mine. Walking hand in hand, we passed many tombstones with their own stories.

We stopped in front of one that read: *Here lies Layla Sunny Carter. Loving wife and mother.*

"I just like to come here sometimes and chop it up with Ma Dukes," he said, looking down at his mother's tombstone. I couldn't begin to imagine the pain he felt.

"She had such a beautiful name," I told him, hugging his tall frame as we stood in silence.

"Yeah, and she was even more beautiful to look at. You're the first person I have ever taken here," he said.

Feeling grateful he chose to share his mother with me, I grabbed him by his waist, and we hugged.

CHAPTER 25

Benny

*E*ver was the first person I had taken with me to my mom's grave. I didn't even think I was mentally prepared to see my daughter's grave yet, so I'd come and visit my mom as much as possible. I didn't know why, but coming here brought me peace. With all the shit that went on in these streets, it'd been hard for me to find a balance.

My daughter used to be that—the only thing that could put the beast in me away when I came home. But with her gone, I just let it roam free inside of me. I, for a long time, just didn't give a fuck. Not a fuck about the bitches I fucked, 'bout the cars I bought, 'bout the lives I took, or even my own life. Having Ever enter my life seemed to be the peace I needed at the moment.

"You never told me how she died, Benny." Ever looked up to me with her eyes full of sadness. I'd hated that shit since I was little—people taking pity on me or feeling sorry for me just 'cause a nigga's momma died.

March 9, 2000...

"Ma, can I have some soda?" I looked up at my mother's deep, mocha skin, and her dimples that I inherited peeked through.

"Now, Benny, you know you need to eat dinner first... but gone get some. Just make sure your daddy doesn't find out." She smiled at me before I ran to the kitchen to get a can of soda.

For the most part, my life was good. My pops, Boe, was a low-level gambler. He made enough for us to get by, and my mom worked odd jobs here and there. We lived in Brownville Houses, and even though we lived in the PJ's, my moms made sure our house was decent.

Sitting at the kitchen table, I watched as my mother paced back and forth. My mother was a religious woman and always claimed to have visions. We never really want to church, although my mother read her Bible faithfully every night.

"Ma, you OK?" I asked as she sat down on the couch.

"Benjamin, come here, please."

I walked to her, and she lifted my head in her hands. Staring into her light brown eyes that matched mine, all I thought about was hoping my future wife be half as beautiful as my mother. Her mocha skin always smelled like roses, and her sisterlocs were always wrapped neatly in a bun on top of her head. My whole life, I'd never witnessed my mother yell, curse, or even fight. Everyone who knew her said just her presence alone made them calm. I guess that trait missed my hot-tempered ass.

"I love you so much, Benny. You know that?" she asked.

"Yeah, Ma, duh." Giggling, I turned my head away from her, but she quickly grabbed it back and looked at me with tears in her eyes. "Mommy, don't cry." Hugging my mother, my six-year-old self was also on the verge of tears.

"I love you so much, Benjamin Glory Carter. I didn't want to name you after Pop Pop, but he died, and I thought it would be a good way to honor my father. I wanted to name you Glory because it filled me with so much joy and pride to have given birth to a child they said I'd never have. Benny, Momma had a bad vision, and hopefully, it's just that. But if it isn't, I just want you to know that I love you with all my soul, and even in your darkest hours, love will guide you home. Home is forever, love." She gave me one kiss, and we never talked about her vision.

A few days later, I awakened to some voices "Why have you come! Please, don't hurt my son!" my mother begged.

"You know what has to be done, Sunny," the unknown voice spoke back.

Peeking out of my bedroom door, I could see my mother's beautiful face wet with tears as her locks hung down her back. A man dressed in all black stood with his back facing me, and at least five masked men stood in my living room along with him.

Her eyes caught mine, and it was as if time itself stopped. Everything my mother wanted to say, she said with her eyes. I saw her pain, rage, and her love as she stared back at me.

"You don't hurt my son," she said, pointing her small finger into the unknown intruder's chest.

"No harm will ever come to the boy, Sunny," he said, calling her by her nickname again.

"Benny, I love—" were her last words as she was cut off by a bullet that pierced into the back of her skull by one of the masked men.

"Leave the boy," the figure said, never turning to face me.

He kneeled over my mother, and once he was done, they left.

"Mommyyyyy! Mom, wake up, please! Mom, don't leave me! Don't leave me here, mom!" I cried.

I peed on myself as I watched my mother take her last breath with the initials B.S. sliced on her cheek.

Life for me after that just got even worse. Boe couldn't be the father I needed him to be and step up. He started messing with heroin and robbing local corner stores. My father was arrested a few months later on the murder of some prostitute, and I soon ended up in a group home. I learned early on that if you didn't stick up for yourself, niggas would try to fuck with you literally and figuratively.

After slicing up this older boy in my bunk, I was sent to solitary.

"Hey. You sliced the shit outta that nigga. Me, I like to poke them," said a little boy with messy braids that looked to be about my age. He looked around, making sure the COs weren't around before flashing me his makeshift shank that looked sharp and dirty as fuck.

Turning my back to him, I stared out the window, wishing it was the men who killed my mother I had sliced instead.

"Hey. I know we don't know each other, but I seen you around. You quiet and keep to yourself. And we look about the same age. And you know niggas is crazy in here," he started to ramble on.

"Yeah." I turned toward him as we each stood in our separate cells.

"Yeah, what?" he asked.

"I'll be your friend." We both grinned at each other and nodded.

After meeting Tru at the group home, my aunt D came to get me a year later and ended up taking Tru as well. She moved us to Flatbush, and that was where we met Lake's goofy ass. And that's how I became feared in these streets.

"MAN, FOREVER, STOP BEING SUCH A BABY." Wiping her tears, I turned to face my momma's tombstone.

"See you later, Ma. I just wanted you to meet my Forever."

CHAPTER 26

Tru

"So, everything is a go?" I asked my bros as we put the last of this month's drug shipment in the back of the van. We had just had our monthly drop-off with that fat fuck Jose. Carlos's ass had still been MIA, and shit wasn't adding up.

"Yeah, bro. Just be on ya shit because that bum Carlos still missing," Benny said, lifting up the last bag of kilos and closing the van door. After getting back to the warehouse and breaking our soldiers off, we decided to head back to my crib to play some 2K18.

"Man, fuck you, Lake. Nigga stays cheating!"

"Oh, shut your ass up and run me my money, Tru." Throwing this nigga ten stacks on his lap, I was done playing his cheating ass.

"So, look. We got this big dinner coming up with Carlos in the next few months. I have a bad feeling about it, so I wanted y'all to be on ya shit until then," Benny said.

Ever since we were young, Benny could sense shit before it happened; before, it used to be weird, but we were so used to it now because he'd always been right.

I got up to get me another beer, and the ringing of my doorbell had all of us reaching for our guns.

"Who the fuck is that?" As I looked through the peephole, my patience was already done. "What the fuck are you doing here, Asia?" I stared at her in an Adidas dress that hugged her ass so right. She looked like she had put on a little weight, but it did her right. It'd been months since I saw her last, and I had to block her ass from calling my phone.

"I missed you, Tru. I haven't seen or fucked you in months! Plus, I needed to talk to you." She pouted. Closing the door, I allowed her to come in.

"Why that thot here?" Benny asked, lifting his head up from the game, while Lake kept his eyes on it.

"Fuck you, Benny," she said.

"No thank you. And don't get fucked up, Asia. I hit birds," this nigga said before turning his attention back to the game.

I pulled her into my bedroom so we could talk. "What the fuck I done told you?"

Pulling at my Glock, I aimed it at her temple. She had me fucked up in many ways. Her showing up to my home unannounced when I'd been dropped her ass was unacceptable.

"Pleaseeee... Tru, I love you. I just missed you." Before she could get out anything else, Lake came barging in.

"Yo, bro, hide that bitch now!" he yelled.

"What, nigga? Why the fuck is you running up in my shit?" I asked, ten seconds away from decking the shit outta of him.

"Man, shut up. Raye, Tay, and E on their way here, like now, nigga!" he said just as my doorbell started to ring. Just then, what he said settled in. If Ray Ray saw this hoe up in my shit, God only knew what would go down.

Pushing her back into my closet, I shoved my gun so far up her mouth that she started to gag as I stared into her frightened eyes." If your ass wanna live to even think about getting this dick again, you better shut the fuck up!" Shoving her ass into my walk-in closet, I closed my room door just as the girls walked in.

"Hey, bro, why you look so stressed?" Ever asked me as she and Taylor embraced me in a hug before joining their men on the couch. Raye took her spot right on my lap.

"Shit, just lost ten racks to this cheating ass nigga Lake, sis. That's all," I replied.

"Well, thank goodness I'm here to make you feel better." Her soft lips locked with mine as we tongued kissed so nastily. We forgot about everyone else.

"Eww... and here I thought Benny was freaky. Y'all nasty!" Ever playfully shoved Raye.

Three hours, four pizza pies, and seven more games of 2K18 later...

"Aye, bros, come help me in the kitchen really quick," I said.

"Nigga, what the fuck I look like? A maid?" Benny's rude ass asked me before his slow ass finally caught on.

"Yo, how the fuck I'mma get Ray Ray to not spend the night?" For the past three hours, all I could think about was hoping the bitch Asia didn't come out the motherfucking closet on some R. Kelly shit.

"Oh shit, I forgot about that girl" Lake broke out in laughter, while my ass was paranoid as fuck.

"Man, nigga, just tell her. Then they can jump that hoe, and I can go home and get my dick sucked," Benny said, taking a seat on my kitchen island.

"Don't worry, bro. I got the best distraction. Trust me," Lake said, turning and walking out of the kitchen. Man, I hoped my boy pulled through for a nigga.

"What the fuck is that smell? Smell like a dead body!" Taylor yelled in disgust. Just then, the most potent smell of just straight up shit came crashing up my nose.

"Yo, what the fuck is that smell! Smelling like a homeless man ass!" Benny turned to me with his shirt over his nose.

"Aye, my bad, bro. I think I may have stopped up your toilet. I think those Hawaiian pizzas ain't agree with me." Lake came strolling into the living room with a look of accomplishment on his face.

"Nah, I'm not staying here. Come on, Tru."

Even though what Lake did was straight up nasty, my dawg came through.

"Ray Ray, go wait out front. I just gotta go get some clothes." After everyone ran out of my spot, I crept back into my room.

After looking down at a sleeping Asia that lay on the floor, I kicked her awake. "Aye, get up and get the fuck out. Asia, if you ever pull this shit again, I'mma fuck you up," I warned.

Walking behind her and gathering my clothes, I made a mental note to call a plumber.

"Oh, wait, I forgot my wallet on the counter," she said. Turning back around, she grabbed her wallet before walking out of my house.

CHAPTER 27

Lake

"OK, that's the last of it," I said, handing Abraham the last stack out of my duffel. We owned several laundromats in both Queens and Brooklyn. Abraham was an old head from around the way that helped us run them.

"How that little lady of yours doing? Bet she is getting big now," he said, closing up the safe that was in the backroom in the laundromat.

"Yeah, man, she is walking now too." Just thinking about my daughter did something to me. She brought me so much life and purpose, and now with Tay Baby, I had to make sure my girls were always straight.

"Listen, man, cherish that shit, especially dealing with the type of baby mama you got. Some bitches are snakes and will hurt the thing you love most in the world all because you ain't love them." He gazed at the wall for a while, in deep thought, I guess.

From all the years I'd known Abraham, he didn't have a wife or kids but, for some reason, always had some good ass advice on them.

"Speaking of crazy baby mamas, I'm 'bout to go have a talk with mines now." Blowing out a breath of frustration, I dapped Abe up and dipped over to Kim's.

I pulled my hood over my locs that were in a bun as I drove through traffic. I brushed a few of my locs out the way that blocked my view. Kim's spot wasn't too far from the wash, so I was there in no time.

Pulling up to Tilden Houses projects, I blew out air in frustration. After dapping up the thirty niggas that stood outside, I climbed six flights of stairs to Kim's crib.

Banging the shit out of her door, I waited as the sounds of locks being turned finally stopped. Kim stood in front of the door, looking every bit like a thick version of Kimora Lee, but that's where her beauty ended.

"Fuck you knocking on my door for, nigga? You lucky I ain't call twelve for kidnapping." She huffed while slamming the door closed.

"Oh, so you the opps now, Kim?" Stepping around her, I made my way into her small ass crib.

I had bought a beautiful house for my daughter and Kim in Jersey, but her hoe ass never cleaned or cooked and always had all her bird friends over.

"I don't like how you came at my girl the other day," I said.

"Nigga, if you ain't have her acting like she Ava's momma, we wouldn't have a problem!"

Looking at the woman that was my child's mother had me ten seconds away from just offing this bitch.

"Why not! Your dumb ass sure doesn't act like Ava's momma. When the last time you called or checked up on her? Kim, you forgot her at daycare and never came back. And now, because my shawty fucking loves my seed as her own, it's an issue?" I asked. "Yo, I only came here because I needed to look you in your eyes so you understand. Ava is no longer your daughter. Kim, if you so much as breathe in her direction ever again, you gonna have a real fucking problem," I warned her before leaving out. Ava's life was better off without Kim in it, but I had a feeling Kim wouldn't think so.

~

"Oh God, Ever... You know she's going to kill that girl," Taylor said on the phone.

Walking into Ava's room, I watched as she ran into Taylor's arms as she talked on the phone.

"Hey, sis, let me call you back. Look, Ava, baby. Daddy's home!" Giving her glossy plum lips a kiss, I took a seat next to her on Ava's bedroom floor.

"Umm, Lake, there something I wanted to ask you." She looked so nervous; Taylor could barely keep eye contact.

"Yeah, sure, go 'head."

"I wanna adopt Ava. We been together for a while, and I know we not married or anything. I just really love this little girl, and I just wanna make sure that I can always be a part of her life. Just in case we don't work out," she spat everything out in one breath.

I wasn't gonna lie; what Tay Baby just asked threw me off. I never fucked with any female that even gave my daughter a second thought. Before Taylor, I never brought any bitch around Ava, because I didn't know if their intentions were pure or not. Everything about Tay just seemed so right, even the part of her I knew she still hid.

"I-I... Wow, Tay, baby."

"No, it's OK. I shouldn't have asked," she said, trying to get up, but I caught her by her left elbow and pulled her on my lap.

"I would love that. Ava fucking loves you, and so do I. And there ain't no 'we ain't gonna work out,' 'cause you stuck with my ass," I said. *Now let's see how my crazy BM takes this.*

CHAPTER 28

Raye

*T*widdling with my thumbs, I was becoming impatient. As I looked at my mark's tracking information, it showed that they would soon be approaching.

"About fucking time," I said to myself.

"Ahhh! Who the fuck is you?" Asia asked as she flicked on her living room light, and there I sat on her couch, dressed in all black. She had on scrubs and had what looked like milk stains on her top.

"Fuck the small talk, bitch. Are you fucking Tru?" Kicking my feet up on her coffee table, I looked back at her, waiting for a response.

"Hoe, I don't know who the fuck you are, but you got the right one today." She started to tie her twenty-six-inch weave up in a ponytail while I sent out a few business e-mails

"I see your ass is slow and can't really understand basic shit. Are you fucking Tru?" this bitch tried to charge me, but before she could get close, I kicked the shit outta her in the stomach, knocking her to the ground. While she lay on the floor, I rained punch on her face. Soon, my fists and brass knuckles were covered in her blood. "So we gonna try this again. *Are you fucking Tru?*" I asked, looking at her.

"No. Nooo. I haven't fucked him in months. I think he turned gay or some shit." After slapping the shit out of her, I stood up and fix myself.

"No, sweetie, he ain't gay. He finally got him some good pussy along with a real bitch," I said.

"Shit, ain't nobody wanted his ass anyway, bitch. Just wanted to talk to his stupid ass! He didn't have to send his guard dog over," she said as she sat up and spat out some more blood.

"Oh, wow, that's good to know. Now I feel less bad about killing your ass," I said to her.

"What you said, bitch?" were her final words as I aimed my .38 at her head and fired.

Who would have thought I would be so wrapped up in a nigga? That I would kill bitches for him? In the time that I got to know Tru, the more I could feel a part of me coming back. I didn't want anything getting in the way of us, and he was lucky he didn't fuck that bitch.

CHAPTER 29

Ever

Sitting at the head of our meeting table, my sisters sat to the left and right of me. Beside them sat our most loyal, ruthless, and trained killers, and at least a hundred or so *Black Skull* members stood in front of us.

"I don't understand. When has it ever been this difficult to find somebody?" Raye asked, speaking lowly to our team. We still weren't any closer on a location for Carlos, and this shit was unacceptable.

"I found out where that nigga at, boss!" said Josh, one of my newest recruits. He was a cutie and looked like he could be Keith Powers' twin. Even though Josh was still in training, he showed himself to have great potential within the organization.

"Well then, speak, Joshie. We ain't got all day," I said, smiling lightly at him, causing him to blush a little.

"Well... one of these crackheads was going on about her son being some big-time kingpin type shit. And saying how she needed to make amends with him and shit. Long story short, she told me how he always has an annual meeting with Carlos," he said. Josh looked back at me as if he had done something good.

"So where is it?" I asked, getting up from my chair and standing in front of his six-four frame.

"Oh, that bitch blacked out after sucking my dick, so I ain't get to ask." His goofy ass smiled and dapped a nigga standing next to him.

"Oh really?" I asked, nodding my head and laughing lightly at the statement he just made.

Revealing my hunting knife like a magician, I stuck it so far through his stomach I felt something burst.

Leaning in close to his ear, I whispered, "Let this be a lesson. Don't ever come at me with only half info. If you ain't got it all, keep that shit to yourself!" I left the knife sticking out of his stomach, my sisters and I left. Don't worry. He lived.

"BENNY, let me go. I gotta pee," I said, shoving his heavy ass off of me. He pulled me tighter into a cuddle as we lay on his bed.

"Fuck you going, Forever! It's three in the morning," he answered, half sleep.

"To the bathroom, stupid." I laughed at how clingy his mean self really was, but I loved it. As I sat on the toilet, Benny's sexy ass came strolling inside in his Polo boxers and sitting down near his big ass Jacuzzi tub.

"Damn, girl, what you ate?" he asked, spraying air fresher.

"Eww, Benny, get out!" I laughed at the faces he was making. There was never a moment I wasn't thinking about or always wanting to be around him. He was my peace. We had grown so attached to one another; it was as if we fed on each other's energy.

"I just feel like I'mma lose you," he said. Looking into his soft, brown eyes, I saw sadness. After wiping and washing my hands, I sat on his lap. I just rested my head on his neck where my name was tatted across it and let the rhythm of his pulse sooth me.

"You're not gonna lose me, poppa. I'm not going nowhere," I assured him.

"I know you ain't, shawty. But if you do, I'll just come find you." He reached behind me and turned on the water. After letting the water fill the tub, we both got in. "So I have a visit with my pops tomorrow," he said as he sat behind me, kissing my neck.

"That's good, Benny. You need to rebuild your relationship with him," I told him.

"Man, fuck that nigga. I'm just going there to get some details on my mom's murder and get justice. Now, enough about that. Turn around and ride me like a surfboard again." He had on the sexiest grin.

I couldn't wait for his dad to give up Benny's mom's killer… so we could kill their asses.

CHAPTER 30

Benny

Six years, four months, and two days was how long it'd been since I'd last seen my pops. Staring back at him from Riker's visiting room, I couldn't help but think, *damn, this nigga looked like me.*

"You look good, son. Heard you out here doing your thing with ya boys." He smirked. My pops was that nigga that always knew what was happening in the hood, even with his ass locked up.

"Yeah, something like that" I said.

"Man, fuck that. My son is that motherfucking nigga in these streets. Shit, you know the COs don't even fuck with me, because they know I'm your pops!" He smiled, showing his two missing front teeth.

Even though I didn't fuck with my pops like that, he was still family. I kept his books heavy and put word out about him being my blood. But I could always sense there was more to him that I didn't know. After my mother's death, he just seemed different and lost control of himself.

"I never got a chance to give my condolences about baby girl," he said, referring to my daughter, Sky. Whenever the topic of my daughter came about, I started to feel uncomfortable, and it was as if my heart started to beat ten times faster.

"No need to. Look, I came to ask if you think or remember any more details on my mother's death," I said, getting straight to the fucking point.

"Man, I never knew you would grow up to be a kingpin, but I still don't think you'll ever beat them," he responded.

"Now, Boe, you and I both know I don't lose. And it's been a minute since you last saw me in action." Leaning forward, I asked, "Who the fuck killed my mother!" I asked.

"The Black Skull. I told you this already; they ain't nobody to mess with. And no matter how big you think you are, they are much bigger. Benny, just let it go."

Getting up from the table, I got my answer and felt there was no need for more talking. I had to prepare for war. My hatred for those motherfuckers ran deep. Yeah, they may be the most feared and deadliest organization ever, but those niggas all bled the same.

CHAPTER 31

Sean "Slice" Jones

I had been watching them for weeks now, watching as they let their guards down and lacked at basic shit. They were living their lives as if they were normal people. Looking at them on the outside, you wouldn't even think they could be so deadly.

But just maybe if they weren't so caught up in those boys, they would have seen me—at the museum where Raye was with some long-haired nigga, maybe when Taylor came waltzing in the mall with her little family, or perhaps if Ever wasn't always following that nigga around in the Lamborghini. They would have seen me. Analyzing them, I became upset with how easy of a target they had become. I sat in their living room in complete darkness and silence with their grandmother that slept peacefully upstairs.

"Damn, Raye, if you and Tru had kissed any longer, y'all would become one," Taylor joked, and her sister's laughter filled the still dark living room.

As if on cue their laughter stopped, and still, the lights were turned off. There they stood in silence with only the dim street lights that helped provide very little light. To an average person, nothing looked or seemed out of the ordinary. But to the three trained killers, I raised. They could hear my light breathing, or even the sound of my eleven million dollar Patek Philippe 1518 watch lightly ticking may have tipped them off.

"Hi, Daddy," my three beautiful daughters said in unison and still in darkness.

"Aw. Y'all don't sound happy to see ya old man." I flicked on the lights, and they each stood before me barely clothed. "Once y'all change, we need to talk," I said to them in a stern voice. Fixing my tailored Versace suit, I took a seat at the head of the table.

"But Daddy, I'm—" Raye started to say, but I cut her off.

"I wasn't asking, Raye." I gave them a serious look, and they turned around and went to change.

"SO WHAT'S NEW?" I asked them while seated at my mother's kitchen table, looking into the eyes of the little snot-nosed girls they once had been and the beautiful and powerful women they were.

"Did you climb through the window again?" Taylor asked as she poured me some of her herbal tea.

"Yeah, baby girl." I smiled at my daughter.

"Girl, you know he is lying. Grandma Tootie let him in." Raye started cracking up. I couldn't do anything but laugh at being caught.

"What do we owe the visit, Daddy?" my baby Ever asked.

From the moment I decided to step down as leader of the Black Skull and give it to my daughters, I had been nothing but proud. I had groomed them for it; my girls were made for this shit.

Everyone had their doubts about if they could handle such a demanding task, but not I. Since they had come into their roles, Raye had opened a new cyber hacking department within the organization. Taylor's street racing team had been a major part in some of the biggest heists the Black Skull had ever done. And Ever's dexterity with guns had helped in the training many new recruits to become some of the deadliest in our organization.

"Well, your mother was worried 'cause y'all haven't checked in, and we wanted to make sure everything was fine." Looking into each of their eyes, I knew a lie was coming in three... two...

"Well, Daddy, I been so busy with school and projects," Taylor lied.

"And me with my internship," Ever said, spitting out hers.

"Yeah, Daddy, and me just living my best life. We kind of got lost in the moment," Raye chimed in.

"Oh, so it wouldn't have nothing to do with Lake Smith, Benjamin Carter, and Tru Wright, now would it?" I asked as looks of shocks showed on their faces.

"How did you find out?" Taylor asked, giving both her sisters nervous glances.

"Y'all got sloppy and comfortable. But none of that matters now. Y'all are to stop this shit at once." I shrugged, dusting off nonexistent dirt off my chest.

"Daddy, you just can't come in here and tell us what to do." Raye shot up from her seat.

"Yeah, that's exactly what I'mma do. Why the fuck is Carlos still missing, huh! Never in Black Skull history has it taken more than forty-eight hours to find someone." Even though I may have stepped down, it didn't mean I wasn't up on shit. Hearing that Carlos's lousy ass hadn't been dealt with yet was intolerable.

"It's getting handled, Daddy. And last I checked, you retired from anything dealing with B.S." My Raye baby came and kissed the top of my bald head.

To say I was a sucker when it came to my daughters would be an understatement. I loved the shit outta them, and they knew how to break me.

"But Daddy, we can still have relationships. I'm in the process of adopting his daughter and—" Taylor said from the across the table.

"Oh, really, Tay? And when are you going to mention that you kill and rob people for a living? Or better yet, how are you going to help raise a child when most of y'all missions take place all over the world!" I roared.

I never thought the day would come where I would question if my children were just a tad bit slow. They knew from the moment they came into power what it instilled—the risk, the loss, and most importantly, the power that came with it. I was barely there to help raise them with my wife because I had to run my organization.

We had acquired a lot of power over the years from politicians to Forbes' top companies and even most of the police department. They were all on our payroll. It was so easy to wipe out enemy teams with cops turning a blind eye.

"Daddy, I love him. He brought back something in me that's been missing for so long. He makes me so happy and is the other part of my soul. Please, Daddy, just give him a chance," Ever said, breaking me from my thoughts.

Ever's tears poured from her beautiful eyes that looked so much like my beautiful wife's. I loved all my children the same, but Ever was special—not because she was biologically mine but because despite the odds against us, she came to be. Everyone always assumed that Taylor was the soft one, but it was really Ever. Just like her mother, she could never turn down being in love.

"Forever, let's not do this again. You remember Devin, don't you? The one you said you loved and that was gonna be with for the rest of your life? The one you decided to reveal all to? The one that ratted us out to the police to save his ass? The nigga that caused us to go to war with the whole fucking police department! The one I made you kill so you know what love truly is! Because, Ever, if it comes down to it, if you loved him, you wouldn't have even pointed the gun to even kill him!" I yelled.

I didn't mean to yell at my daughter, but at times, she could be so stubborn. She especially had to let this new nigga go. ASAP.

"He's different, Dad," she softly spoke, getting up to leave.

My words stopped her. "This is your warning, Ever. Either y'all stop entertaining these niggas and get focused, or y'all can just go visit them in the cemetery."

Taking one last look back at me, she left her sisters and me.

"But, Daddy," Raye whined while pulling on my arm like she did when she was a little girl who always wanted her way.

"Raye, please trust me. Y'all could never be. Raye, baby girl, you barely even know who you are. How could you girls expect what y'all have with them to work? Huh?" Getting frustrated, I kissed my girls goodbye, and I left, praying my daughters took my warning—not because I didn't want them to find love, but why did it have to be with these niggas? I prayed they took my advice. But knowing my daughters, I knew they wouldn't.

CHAPTER 32

Raye

I wasn't gonna lie. What my father said about me not knowing myself kinda hurt a bit. For almost two years, I'd been working hard on trying to regain my memory of before I was adopted. There were no traces of me beforehand in any national databases I had hacked so far. The closest I'd come to having my memory back was when I was with Tru.

"OK, Raye. Same time, same place," Dr. Thomas said as she closed her notepad. We had made so much progress in my memory retrieval. I found myself having bits of flashbacks of events that I never recalled occurring.

"OK, T. I feel really good about this session. Like I'm a step closer to finding myself," I said.

"That's so great to hear! You should also bring Tru then next time you come. I would love to have him here with you," she said as she held open her office door for me.

Besides my family, no one else knew of my visit with Dr. Thomas, and I wanted to keep it that way.

"Yeah, I don't know about that, T. How does it look, asking him to come to my therapist office?" Dr. Thomas had already suggested bringing Tru in, but I was too afraid to admit my truth to him. How could I? It was bad enough he didn't know about what I did for a living, but add that to me having fucking amnesia. I figured I'd hold off on telling him.

Leaving out of her office, I headed down into Midtown to have dinner with Red. He had been calling me nonstop. And even though I knew I shouldn't be meeting him, there my ass was.

"Damn, Raye, you look fine as fuck, shawty," he said as soon as I walked up to the table. He wasn't lying either; I kept it cute in a red floral dress and a pair of vans Tru got me to match his. Taking me by surprise, he pulled out my seat for me. Tru had already gotten me used to things like that, but with Red's ass, I would be lucky if he told me "God bless you" when I sneezed.

"You know this the first time we ever want out to eat?" I asked more to myself than him. It had just dawned on me how Red's trifling ass never even took a bitch out to eat. There was no really comparing Red and Tru, because they definitely weren't the same. Tru took me out, talked to me about everything, and made me laugh so much with his corny ass jokes.

"Shit, Raye. Give a nigga a break. We here now, right?" He reached for my hands across the table. Feeling uncomfortable, I grabbed them back and pulled out my phone to avoid the awkwardness.

"I guess. Look, I can't stay long. What you wanna talk about?" Tru and I were meeting up later to head to the movies, so Red had to hurry the fuck up.

"Damn, it's like that? Well, I wanna know what's going on with us. One minute, you my bitch, and then the next, you acting brand new on a nigga. You know I love your ass," he said, flashing his gold grill and looking like he could be Chris Brown's long-lost brother. I really did love Red, or so I thought. Maybe it was more so his swag, and damn, did this nigga have it. But then came Tru, and Red didn't even hold a candle to his swag. It got me wet just from thinking about him.

"Look, Red, what we had was good or whatever, but it's over now.

I realized that you're not the nigga for me." Looking across the table at him, I could see that he wasn't feeling what I had just said.

"Fuck you talking about, Raye! We were fucking good when your ass was back in the A. You ain't fucking leaving me, Raye. I put that on everything," he said, knocking my red wine over.

"Nigga, now I know you got me fucked up. Listen, it was a mistake in me coming here. Just leave me alone, Red." Shooting up outta my seat, I was already seconds always from blowing his head off. Literally.

Turning quickly around, I said. "For your sake, just let this go, Red. Move on. Plus, if my nigga finds out about you harassing me, he'll fuck you up." With that, I headed toward my baby's house.

CHAPTER 33

Tru

"Thanks so much for your help, Aunt D." I looked at my aunt's smiling face as we Facetimed, and she walked me through the famous meatloaf recipe. I had gone all out for tonight with Raye. Her birthday was in a few weeks, but we had a huge meeting going on that day, so I had to put something together in the meantime.

"Look at my Tru boo, over there cooking for a girl. I taught my boys good." After finishing my call with my aunt, I hopped in the shower.

Putting my freshly washed hair into a bun, I opted to keep my outfit simple. My all-black Balenciaga sweater and jeans paired with my space jams put my fit together.

Hearing the jiggling of keys, I rushed and put on Daniel Caesar's "Get You" to play in the background. I looked at a shocked Raye, who looked to be on the verge of tears. The lyrics of the songs really spoke to me.

Every time I look into your eyes, I see it.
You're all I need. Every time I get a bit inside, I feel it.

Ooh, who could've thought I'd get you? Ooh, who would've thought I'd get you?

"Babe! You did all this for me?" She hugged my neck so tight I felt her tears drop down my neck.

Looking at the rose petals I had scattered throughout the house, she followed them into the kitchen where I had dinner set up.

〜

"So did you like it? Your surprises?" I asked Raye as we lay on my couch, watching an episode of *Power*.

"Like? Tru, I loved it. And I am so grateful for everything you did for me," she said, kissing my lips. I always knew that when I got myself a girl, I would treat her right. Besides Aunt D, I didn't really have a woman to teach me how to treat one, because my own momma was out in the streets hoeing.

"Come on, Ray Ray. Don't go crying on a nigga again. I just wanted to show you that I love you and wanna be with you. I ain't coming to you on no soft nigga shit either. I'm coming to you as a man, Raye. I want this. I want us. I want to one day make you my wife and knock you up with as many kids as possible. No games, just real shit." Pulling her up into my lap, I stared into her face, a face I felt like I'd seen before.

"Thank you, Tru, for going that extra mile and showing how you feel about me. And I promise to give you all of me." Hearing that, I lifted her up in the air with her legs still strapped around me. Never breaking our kiss, I carried her into the bedroom where I lay her on the bed, ready to go overtime on that pussy.

Pulling her purple lace panties down, I stare at her neatly trimmed landing strip that led straight to her pussy.

"Come here, bae," she said, crawling toward me on all fours, letting her ass jiggle with each movement.

Unzipping my pants, she took out my dick from my Polo boxers. She started at the tip of my dick, lightly licking my head and spitting on it. Once she had my shit really wet, she was bopping up and down like a pro. Grabbing the back of her head, I fucked her mouth. She surprised me by not gagging, instead taking that shit like a pro.

We fucked and made love for the rest of the night. Staring at a sleeping, naked Raye that lay in bed beside me, I just felt a sense of familiarity.

"Why do I feel like I know you, Ray Ray?" I whispered in her ear. She stirred a little but didn't wake up. Giving her one more kiss, I pulled her into my chest.

CHAPTER 34

Benny
A Few Weeks Later...

*T*he business had been booming legally and illegally. We had opened two more barbershops and were almost finished with opening our own fucking McDonald's down in Flatbush. But that drug game, we had on lock. We had doubled up our product from that bitch ass Carlos, and he couldn't even keep up with our demands.

"Alright, so, boom, that nigga Xian willing to meet with us. But that nigga wants us on the next flight to Thailand ASAP, bro," Tru said, passing me the blunt. We were at my spot, going over a few details for a meeting with Carlos in a few days.

"Damn, bro, if we get shit popping with Xian, we are going to be on a different level." Xian was this Asian dude who had access to poppy fields out in Thailand that were used to make heroin, the purest kind ever. If we were to get right with him, we could cut out that middleman like Carlos's bitch ass and go straight to that source to triple our profit.

"Yeah, bro, once we have this final meeting with Carlos, that shit will definitely be a go," I said.

"Yo, you heard about Asia's ass getting knocked?" I looked at Tru, and he seemed really surprised by the news, which in turn surprised me because I thought his ass was the one that killed her.

"Fuck you mean, Asia got knocked?" he asked, surprised.

"Man, her mama came by the courts the other day, bawling her eyes out, talking about they done killed her baby. Said she was shot in the crib and that the police have no leads." Taking a bite of my chopped cheese, I studied him as his faced filled with different emotions.

"Damn, shawty was type crazy. Shit, I guess she fucked with the wrong nigga," he said.

They chilled for a little bit longer before I kicked their asses out and went and scooped Forever up.

A Few Hours Later...

"OK... you can look now," Ever said, turning over her sketchbook. She drew a faceless woman that had two different faces on both sides of her. The face on her right looked soft and pure, almost innocent. The face on the left seemed dark; her eyes were black, and her facial expression looked hard.

"Damn, baby girl, this shit is dope. Can I have it?" I asked, grabbing the drawing form her hand.

"Really! Yeah, you can. I just have to fix some of the linings," she said as she started to redo her line work.

"Is that you, Forever?" I asked.

There'd always been a part of me that felt that Ever was holding back, not only about her but even in our relationship. She was always so guarded with herself. Shit, if I didn't walk in on her a few weeks ago drawing, I wouldn't have even known that my girl could draw her ass off.

"Huh? Umm, maybe. I don't know," she said, twirling one of her curls; she always seemed to do that when she got stressed.

Lifting her head and looking into those hazel eyes, I saw the hurt she tried so hard to hide. Her eyes began to water over, and before long, tears fell from her beautiful eyes. Not knowing what the fuck made her cry, I grabbed her into my arms.

"He really hurt me bad, Benny," she mumbled, her face still buried in my chest.

"Who the fuck hurt you, Ever? Huh! I swear on everything, I'mma kill him," I said.

She had the nerve to smirk, knowing damn well that I was deadass.

"Not like that, Benny. My ex. He made it so hard to trust someone. He made it so hard to fall in love again, but I did. With you. I trusted him, and he just made a fool of me. It keeps replaying in my mind, and I don't wanna lose you, Benny. He just hurt me so bad," she said, bawling her eyes out now.

"Listen to me, Forever, because this is the last time you will ever cry to me about a next nigga. You can't compare me to no nigga, baby girl, 'cause every last one of them will fall short. Forever, I have to know now if you're ready to close that chapter and start a new one with me. I promise to be everything he wasn't and then some. Just have faith in me, and I won't let you down," I said to her truthfully.

One thing I hated more than anything was when people weren't true—to themselves or others. I knew there was more to Ever than what she let on, but I was willing to overlook that... for the time being. But what I couldn't overlook was my shawty crying over a next nigga while in my face.

"OK, Benny. I trust you with everything in me. And I promise to not let my past interfere with us anymore," she said, wrapping her arms around my neck. She started to lick and kiss all over the spot where I tatted her name.

"Cool. Now get naked. Oh, and wipe the snot off your face," I said, removing my shirt and untying my sweats.

"Wait. Benny, there something I gotta tell you," she tried to say.

"Fuck it. Keep the snot. You're still pretty." Wasting no time, I picked her up, threw her over my shoulder, and headed to the bedroom to punish my pussy.

CHAPTER 35

Ever

"$\mathcal{I}$ see Benny copped you that new Bentley truck. So, when you gonna tell him you got two of those already?" Raye asked as we all sat around our office in our warehouse in Lower Manhattan.

We were finalizing our plan for Carlos. The crackhead Josh mentioned had come through with some useful information. I planned on getting rid of her junkie ass once she gave us the drop, but something in my gut told me to let her live.

"I was but got sidetracked by the D." Both of my sisters stared, looking at me, surprised by my response. Shit, I even surprised myself. Ever since our talk, I'd been thinking of ways to tell him who I really was.

"Oh my God! Really, Forever? Then we'll be able to tell them all about who we are. You must really be crazy about that nigga," Taylor said, hugging from behind.

"Shit, I never thought I'd see the day that Forever Marie Jones would tell another soul she is one of the leaders of the Black Skull."

These hoes started to applaud me, and then I just had to leave out the office.

Walking a few rooms toward the back, I pulled out a key ring. After stopping in front of the room, I found the key and inserted it into the keyhole and entered.

"How are you holding up, Isis?" I asked her as she lay down on the bed, watching TV.

Isis was the crackhead that gave us the information on Carlos. My sisters, especially Raye, both thought it would be better if I had killed her. But something in my heart told me not to, and because of that, I was the one responsible for her.

"Hey, baby. I'm doing much better than I was a few days ago." She smiled back.

Isis was a beautiful woman once cleaned up. She had the silkiest hair I'd ever seen, and she barely needed to wash it.

"Yeah, detoxing does that. I'm going to have the doctor come over later to take your vitals. And if he tells me everything is good, I might have Chef Troy whip you up more of that tuna salad you like," I offered.

"You trying to get me thick, huh? Can I ask you something?" she asked, sitting up in her bed. I had bought her new clothes; no one would have ever guessed that, weeks before, she was a strung-out crackhead.

"Um, sure." Taking a seat at the end of the bed, I waited for her to speak.

"Why you helping me? One minute, I'm sucking Josh dick in the alley, and then the next, I ended up here. You feed me, clothe me, and shit, I ain't never seen the doctor as much as I do here, but why?" she asked

"I don't know. My father told me a long time ago that you should give people a chance to show their true self. Because they might just be kind, trustworthy people. And if they aren't... you kill them." Winking at her, I got up and headed for the door.

"Who-who are you?" she asked.

I paused, surprised by her question. Giving her one last smile, I left out without answering her.

~

AFTER COUNTLESS MONTHS of searching for Carlos, we had gathered intel of his whereabouts. Our private jet was already prepared for our departure. It worked out perfectly because the guys would be out of town around the same time as us, and we could get back without them noticing.

"He's been spotted going into his beach house in Miami, boss," Ricky, one of my lieutenants, said as I came walking down the stairs.

"Great. Make sure we don't lose contact with him. Have Nickel's team patrol there until we get there," I said.

"Sure thing, E. See y'all in Miami. Going out there a day early to partake in some extracurricular actives," he said, winking at us before leaving.

"Bitch, keep playing on my phone. You'll see how bad you are when I slice your fucking gut open!" Taylor yelled into her phone before slamming it on the counter. See, people thought I was the crazy one, but it was really Taylor's ass.

"Who the fuck was that, sis?" I asked.

"Lake's simple ass baby mother has been playing on my phone for a week straight. She really gonna make me revert back to my old ways." She huffed before taking a pull of the blunt we had in rotation.

"Well, baby, get to reverting. 'Cause, sis, she is trying you, and she is playing with the wrong ones. I've been itching to try out this new potassium chloride poison. Have her insides burning the fuck up," Raye said, typing away on her laptop.

"Nah, it's cool. I will definitely handle her when we get back," she said, blowing out smoke.

Later That Day...

"You gonna miss poppa while he's gone?" Benny asked as he had me bent over on his desk, hitting it so right from the back.

"Ohhhh, yes, poppa. I'mma miss you so fucking much," I moaned as he held my arms back and continued to pound into me. A few moments later, we came together, and after showering, we lay in the bed naked.

"You're sure you don't wanna come with me? You might like where I'm going," Benny said as I lay on his chest and listened to the rhythm of his heart while he played in my hair.

Already, I was missing him, and we hadn't even left yet. I had contemplated sitting this one out and having my sisters handle it without me. Don't get me wrong. Being a leader of the B.S. did have its perks, but having to be away from your loved ones sucked the most.

"Nah. Me and my sisters have something plan for Raye's birthday, so it's fine. Just come back to me as soon as you can." Rubbing his waves, I couldn't help but kiss his lips.

"Yeah, I ain't even leave yet, and I already miss your ugly ass." He kissed my forehead as we lay in silence for a while. A feeling of loss swept through me, so I held on tighter to him. It could have just been nerves, but somehow, I knew it was more.

"Oh, you never told me how it went with your father," I said.

"He basically just confirmed what I knew for a while now. That the Black Skull killed my mom, and he's against me trying to start a war with them. But fuck them! I'm coming for every last one of them niggas 'til I get to the leaders; they killed my mother, so I'm laying everybody the fuck out," he said with much assurance.

My heart literally stopped beating. Hearing him say those words almost had me about to faint. Were we the cause of his mother's death? This couldn't be fucking happening. How could I have not known? I felt ill just at the thought of it.

"Man, Forever, I promised to not be gone that long. No need to be crying on a nigga." Not even realizing that I was crying, I quickly wiped them up. Giving me one last kiss, he pulled me close to his chest.

"Benny. I... I... I..."

All that could be heard were his light snores. As he wrapped his arms around me tightly, I thought about the man I had fallen in love and how sleeping next to him usually brought me peace. But as I looked at him, I knew that our lives would change.

CHAPTER 36

Raye "Keyz"

"**E**verything is a go. His security systems are a joke," I boasted to my team as we sat a few houses down from Carlos's house. There was nothing that brought me more excitement than sitting on my laptop and hacking into someone's security systems; this object was supposed to be their defense against something dangerous, but sadly, it just helped in their demise.

A black minivan pulled up beside me. Its darks tint made it difficult to see who the occupants were. The passenger side window, the one closest to my side, slowly rolled down. Taylor's cute face peeked through with a freshly lit blunt in her mouth. Ever was seated in the driver's seat, while Ricky and two other loyal B.S. members sat in the back.

"Raye, how are we looking?" Taylor asked me, leaning out of the car window.

"I just got into his security system, which was quite easy by the way; once I broke the cameras firewall, configured his I.P. range, started a scan to find out where the CCTV cameras were, I was able to—"

"Keyz, Keyz, we get it. They don't call you *Keyz* for nothing. So, I'm guessing we good?" Ever asked, cutting me off from finishing my very informative speech.

"Damn, C.P., let a bitch have her moment. But yes, we're in. His cameras are all now in a loop of old footage," I said.

"Speeder, I need you to double check your men at the entrance. Make sure all their cars are out of sight," Ever ordered.

"Oh shit! Y'all, we have a problem," I said to my sisters. While looking over Carlos's security cameras, I saw all too familiar faces.

CHAPTER 37

Carlos

"Hey! Jose, make sure we have guys covering the front and back of the house at all times!" I yelled to Jose's fat ass as he walked away while barking commands into a walkie-talkie.

I wasn't worried about the motherfuckers I had a meeting with later on that night. I was worried about the fucking Black Skull coming for my neck all because I broke the rule of no killing of kids and ended up killing three-year-old twin girls because their cracked-up parents owed me two hundred dollars... Hey, it wasn't about the money; it was about respect.

Benny and his brothers were one of my best business associates. These dudes brought me too much money. I had no choice but to come out of hiding and meet with them.

"They're pulling up now, boss," Jose said, closing my office door. Looking through my security cameras, I saw a black Cadillac pull up and them exiting the car. My security cameras went black for a second before suddenly turning back on. After making sure my camera system was fine, I left out of my office.

"Gentlemen, it's so good to see you all." Each one of them ignored my hand that I held out for a shake. Instead, they walked into my living room and sat at my table.

"You guys have been killing it these last couple of months. My connect will be able to resupply us in a few days or so," I informed them.

"Man, first the fuck off, where ya ass been at, Carlos? You seem mad sus' right now," Tru said, a few seats away from me. His brothers looked at me, waiting for an answer.

"Come on, guys. You know how it goes. Got caught up with some things, but I'm here now."

My butler came up and poured each of us a drink. I was far from a weak man, but this meeting really had me on edge. They sat at the table, not drinking or talking. They just stared at me.

"Man, your bitch ass lying. But it's cool. The only reason we here is to get the rest of the product you owe us. Oh yeah and to let you know your services are no longer needed," Benny said, looking me dead in my eyes.

CHAPTER 38

Benny

"Fellas, come on. Let's talk about this." Carlos threw his hands into the air. Everything about this meeting seemed off from the extra security and Carlos's ass looking all paranoid. Cutting ties with this nigga was the best decision for us now more than ever.

"Man, let's just go," Lake said, standing up and waiting for Tru and me.

"Come on, guys. We can work something—" That was the last thing Carlos said before all the lights in the mansion went out.

As if instinctively, Lake, Tru, and I all pulled our guns outs. At least ten of Carlos's men came and surrounded him, guarding him like the fucking president.

"Don't let them kill me!" he yelled behind them. The next thing I knew, niggas came from everywhere on some ninja shit. Masked men dressed in all black came crashing through windows and knocking down doors. We all just started letting off on these niggas, but they just seemed endless. We would kill two, and twenty more would come through the door.

"Yo, stay fucking close!" I yelled to my bros, looking to my left and right to where they stood. We were holding our own, but Carlos had maybe three niggas left... Shit, he was down to one.

"Aye, yo. Ya notice that these niggas ain't even shooting at us?" Lake asked, still firing at those niggas even though they were more focus on Carlos and his crew.

"Shit, I'm out!" Tru yelled.

"Me too, bro," I said, letting off my last bullet into a nigga's skull. I got into my fighting stance, ready to lay a motherfucker out. But still, these niggas acted as if we weren't in the room. Once they laid out all of Carlos's boys, they shot him once in his leg and tied him up before carrying him out. The lights in the mansion came back on, and all the dead bodies came into view.

"Our bosses would like a word with you all," one of the masked men said. We stood in a bloody room with at least fifty armed niggas, and we didn't have any idea what the fuck was going on. The sound of doors opening from behind caused me to turn around.

I was mad as shit to see Forever, Raye, and Taylor walk through the door.

"Forever, you good, baby? Them niggas hurt you?" I asked, rushing to her. I made sure she didn't have a hair out of place.

"Why the fuck ya kidnap our girls for? Fuck is going on?" Tru yelled, decking the shit out of one of the masked me.

"Benny, there's something I gotta tell you. And I just want you to know that I love you so much," Ever said to me as her sisters stood to her side. She had tears streaming down her face. This day was beyond confusing.

"Man, can't that shit wait, Forever? We got to get the fuck outta here," I said.

"No. We... we-we. My name is Ever Marie Jones," she said, trying her hardest to get her words out.

"I know that already, baby, born May 25, 1994. Your favorite color is purple, and you love to draw. Forever, what the fuck does that have to do with anything?" I asked.

"And my sisters and I are the leaders of the Black Skull," she said, barely able to look at me in the eyes.

"What the fuck? Tay, you a fucking assassin?" Lake blurted out.

"I knew your ass was a sniper, Ray," Tru said to Raye as I still tried to digest what had just been said.

I was really getting pissed off that they thought it would be funny to joke at this moment. We had dead niggas and niggas around us with guns for Christ's sake.

"Tell me you are playing, Forever," I said after realizing that she didn't say it was a joke yet.

"Benny, please hear me out. I wanted to tell you."

"Nah, you are playing. I know you not trying to tell me that you're a part of something that killed my mother."

She tried to reach for me, but I aimed my gun that had one more bullet in it at her head. Her hand glided over the gun on her waist before dropping them to her sides. She stared at me with those eyes that I loved to look at and pressed her head to the gun.

"Benny, please. I wanted to tell you, but I couldn't. I didn't want to lose you. I love you so much. It's me. Please," she begged as I tried to think if I could kill her and still make it out of there alive.

One of the masked men raised his gun at me.

"Don't ever raise a gun to him! Do you understand!" Ever shouted, shooting the man in the hand. Nodding his head, he doubled over in pain.

"Benny, please, just listen," she said.

"Get the fuck off me, bitch! If you as so much as come near me again, I will fucking kill you. I hate you! You ain't shit to me but a bitch that lied to me and killed my mother." Her hurt face meant nothing to me.

Walking past everyone, I left, not stopping. I just kept on walking, thinking about how this trip went from business to me losing the only thing I had left that I genuinely loved... *Forever.*

NOTE FROM AUTHOR

If you thought book one was lit, don't worry. Book two will be even better. I had so much fun bringing these characters to life! I think I made them each to be a piece of something I wish to be. Ever began both deadly and soft. Raye was always looking to turn up but was smart as fuck. And Taylor was in tune with her spiritual side.

Should book two focus more on just the girls, or do you guys enjoy learning about our fellas as well? Let me know! And see ya soon.

— SADÈ IONA

ABOUT THE AUTHOR

Sade is a 26-year-old mother of an amazing one-year-old son; who resides in Bronx NY. She also had a passion for writing from a young age. From writing school plays, and new articles she always found new ways to express herself through her words. Recently signing with Royalty has opened new opportunities and now others can now experience her work on a bigger platform.

facebook.com/sade.iona.7

instagram.com/sade_iona

Royalty Publishing House is now accepting manuscripts from aspiring or experienced urban romance authors!

WHAT MAY PLACE YOU ABOVE THE REST:

Heroes who are the ultimate book bae: strong-willed, maybe a little rough around the edges but willing to risk it all for the woman he loves.

Heroines who are the ultimate match: the girl next door type, not perfect - has her faults but is still a decent person. One who is willing to risk it all for the man she loves.

The rest is up to you! Just be creative, think out of the box, keep it sexy and intriguing!

If you'd like to join the Royal family, send us the first 15K words (60 pages) of your completed manuscript to submissions@royaltypublishinghouse.com

LIKE OUR PAGE!

Be sure to <u>LIKE</u> our Royalty Publishing House page on Facebook!